SLAVE

by
Rosetta Stone

SILVER MOON BOOKS LTD
PO Box CR 25 Leeds LS7 3TN
SILVER MOON BOOKS INCORPORATED
PO Box 1614 New York NY 10156

New authors welcome

Printed and bound in Great Britain

*Silver Moon Books of Leeds and New York
are in no way connected with Silver Moon Books of London*

If you like one of our books you will probably like them all!
For free 20 page booklet of extracts from our first 16 books (and, if you wish to be on our confidential mailing list, from new monthly titles as they are published) please write to:-

Silver Moon Reader Services
PO Box CR 25 Leeds LS7 3TN
or
PO Box 1614 New York NY 100156

Surely the most erotic freebie ever!!

SLAVE TO THE STATE copyright 'Rosetta Stone'
First published 1996

SLAVE TO THE STATE

Rosetta Stone

This is fiction - in real life practice safe sex

Chapter One

Waiting was the hardest part. Waiting, and avoiding looking at the wicked collection of whips and canes hanging so pointedly from the bedpost.

She could hear the sounds of her lover as he showered in preparation for what lay ahead. There was no need for him to shower but she guessed that he enjoyed prolonging the anticipation.

He wasn't really her lover, none of them were, not in the usual sense of he word, but Julia found it easier to think of him that way. She thought of all the men she served as her lovers, as if by doing so she could excuse the beatings and abuse she suffered at their hands. The shower stopped and she stiffened, eyes fixed on the bathroom door, heart beginning to beat faster as it opened...

Now she stood before him, marvelling at the casual power he exercised over her. Already she could feel the lips of her sex moistening, her nipples swelling hard as her breathing quickened.

It always affected her like that. She could never stop her arousal from happening, no matter how hard she tried.

She wasn't naked. Not yet. But soon now, very soon, he would order her to strip off her thin, silk robe, then her sheer stockings and suspender belt and finally her tiny lace panties. She would strip slowly, peeling each item away as enticingly as she knew how, careful to please her lover of the moment, eager to please him, to avoid punishment if she could...

But punishment was his thing. That was what they all

wanted her for, to punish her.

"Get on with it!"

His tone was sharp, impatient, and Julia responded quickly. Spreading her legs well apart, she reached for the ceiling, up onto her toes, raising both arms above her head and crossing her wrists as though to be restrained. As her body stretched, the thin silk of her robe pulled tight against her firm curves, clinging to the proud thrust of her breasts and buttocks, outlining her nipples.

"Higher!"

Again the sharpness in his command and again she responded. The muscles in her legs strained and quivered as she rose right up onto her toes and pushed her arms higher and straighter. She breathed deeply and evenly, limbs quivering with the tension of holding the pose as he walked slowly around her, inspecting her from every angle until at last he faced her again. Her breasts jutted boldly against their silken covering and though she held her head high she was aware of him reaching out for them.

His touch was like a shock rippling through her and she forced herself to remain still as he cupped and fondled each firm swelling mound, fingers circling almost lazily around her nipples, stroking and teasing. Her body responded, the tight buds swelling even more and throbbing with each touch until she could contain herself no longer and moaned softly, swaying forward.

Satisfied, he slid his hand further down her body, slipping them under the belt of her robe. Pausing for a few moments he gazed into her face, reading her growing arousal in her half closed eyes and parted lips and then he pulled outwards, slipping the loose knot free. The belt fell away and Julia's robe opened, the thin silk whispering across the swell of her breasts like a curtain opening on her nakedness.

He did not touch her now, even though her breasts jutted out, offered up for his pleasure. Her nipples thrust out inviting and dark against the pale tan of her smooth skin. Her whole body trembled. Already she was on fire, wanting him to touch her, caress her, use her, wanting against all her strivings.

He stepped behind her and reached up to grasp her arms, bringing them down by her side and then releasing her to slip the robe away from her shoulders. The silk heaped on the floor about her feet and Julia waited until her arms were grasped again, brought together behind her back and pulled sharply down. Her back arched under the sudden strain and her belly thrust forward. He pressed against her, so close that she could feel his breath on her neck. So close that her pinned hands brushed against the swelling of his erection. So close that he could reach around and press his fingers against the tight damp lace of her panties.

She gasped and squirmed at his touch, feeling his fingers tracing the now sharply defined outline of her sex, sliding insistently back and forth. Her arousal was growing with each new touch, the scent of it heavy in the air around her as she felt herself opening under his caress. Moaning gently, she surrendered herself to her lover, parting her thighs wider and leaning back against him as he fondled her.

Abruptly he pushed her away and she staggered, almost losing her balance until he grasped her arm, urging her towards the bed.

"Bend over. Keep your legs open."

Almost sobbing with frustration, her body still quivering with arousal, Julia obeyed. She spread her legs wide and in one smooth movement, bent forward in the way she knew her lover desired. Her outstretched arms supported her and her breasts hung down beneath her. Her panties clung wetly to the still swelling lips of her sex and she was suddenly glad of the low lighting of the bedroom to hide her shame as she waited anxiously for him to touch her again.

He moved quickly, taking her by surprise.

His hands closed around her firmly rounded buttocks, sliding up inside her panties, bunching up the thin fabric and pulling it tightly up into the crease of her backside. Julia gasped and lifted up onto her toes. The sudden tension between her thighs opened her wider and the tightly bunched lace was drawn irresistibly up between the wet throbbing lips. Her lover watched, increasing the tension more and more and bedding the twisted lace deeper and deeper into her until she squirmed and writhed helplessly beneath him. He whipped her then, grabbing a short leather strap from the bedpost and swinging it down hard and without warning.

Thwack!
Thwack!
Thwack!

Sharp, stinging strokes, delivered without respite or heed to Julia's shocked gasps.

Thwack!
Thwack!
Thwack!

There was no escape for as she twisted and bucked under the onslaught, her lover kept a firm grip on her panties.

Thwack!
Thwack!
Thwack!

With each stroke that whipped in he increased the tension, jerking her quivering bottom up to meet the stinging leather, and Julia could do nothing to prevent it. Her bottom burned under the seemingly relentless thrashing and each new tug on her panties bedded them deeper inside her sex, opening her wider and wider and sending uncontrollable spasms of arousal racing through her belly.

Thwack!
Thwack!
Thwack!

As suddenly as it had begun the flogging ceased and the pressure between her thighs was eased, leaving her trembling once more. Her body was drenched with perspiration and her breasts heaved beneath her as she fought her breathing back under control. Her backside was on fire but her sex gaped and a fire of a very different kind burned in her belly, the juices betraying her arousal soaking into her now ruined panties.

Throwing the strap aside, he slid onto the bed and knelt between her outstretched arms. His own robe was now fully open, his erection thrusting towards her. No orders were needed. Julia sucked in a deep breath and leaned forward to take him into her mouth.

Slowly, she sucked the thick, throbbing shaft between her lips and her lover leaned forward into her, reaching under to grasp her swaying breasts. Drawing her towards him he penetrated deeper into her mouth, sighing with satisfaction as she worked busily on him until she was forced to pull back, gasping for breath. Now when she bent for him she held him just inside her lips, teasing him with quick, darting flicks of her tongue. Twisting her head to one side she trailed her lips wetly up and down the length of him, feeling the slow pulses building inside.

A shudder rippled through him and he grasped for her, guiding her back to the swollen head of his cock. She understood at once, she had been well taught, she strained her lips wide once more and drew him back into her mouth. His hands returned to her breasts, gripping harder as his climax built, squeezing the throbbing buds of her nipples until she too shuddered.

Deep inside her lover's cock she felt a sudden surge and reared back, gasping one last deep breath before plunging down onto him once more, lips clamped tightly around his hot, pulsating flesh.

"Yes ... good ... yes ... YES ..."

Julia's head was moving steadily, lips sliding smoothly up and down his straining shaft, working him without pause as his climax built and burst. She could feel the pressure growing inside him, funnelling rapidly into the tight confines of his cock. His breath quickened, his hands on her breasts clutching tighter and then he swelled even harder, straining her lips wider and spattered her throat with thick jets of sperm.

Clamping her lips around him as he gasped and shuddered above her, she felt her mouth fill with the hot creamy taste of him and sucked urgently as she felt small dribbles escaping and trickling down her chin.

His spasms eased and she slipped him loose from her mouth, swallowing hard, the taste of him sharp and lingering in her throat. His erection was shrinking rapidly and she swallowed hard once more before bending to draw him between her lips, sucking the last salty residue from his softening shaft and licking him clean until he ordered her to stop. She lay still, holding him between her lips until he pulled back from her and sprawled lazily across the bed.

"Stand up."

Slowly, careful not to inflame the sting of her thrashing, Julia rose to her feet and assumed her former position. She was very conscious now of the jutting hardness of her nipples, while her panties, still pulled hard up between her legs drew attention to the swelling gape of her sex.

"Naked!"

Without a word, Julia dropped her arms to unclip her suspenders, raising each foot onto the bed in turn as she slowly worked each stocking down her legs. Reaching behind she unclipped the suspender belt itself, the action tightening her shoulders so that her breasts thrust forward. Her lover let his gaze linger on her proud display and she held the ends of the belt behind her back, stiffening her shoulders even more until he nodded briefly and she let the scrap of lace fall to the floor.

She was caught up in her actions, knowing how much they were exciting him. As seductively as she knew how, she slid her hands down her body, slipping them easily under the waistband of her panties and easing them across her hips. A quick shake of her hips and they slipped loose and she stepped free to stand naked, legs spread and arms raised as before.

He lay back, his eyes roaming slowly over her body, very pleased with what he saw. Julia was just twenty two, blonde and a little over five and a half feet tall. She was slim but with full well rounded breasts, the nipples large and deep red and even when not swollen with arousal as they were now, always half erect. Her belly was flat and firm, making the swell of her pubic mound seem even more pronounced and inviting and her mound was shaved smooth. Between her slender thighs, parted now at his wish, the lips of her sex were swollen and puffed up, not just from her aroused condition but from frequent attention from 'lovers'.

A man tearing his attention from her charms to look into her face would note wide blue eyes and a generous mouth, always ready to smile but half open now, lips parted with desire.

"Get up onto the bed."

Rolling aside, he made room for Julia to take his place and she scrambled eagerly up, kneeling with her hands behind her back.

"Arms out in front."

Julia held her arms straight out in front and her lover bent to pick up the discarded belt from her robe. Quickly and efficiently he looped it round each of her wrists, knotted it tightly in between and secured the loose end to the bed frame. It was a simple but effective tether, pinning her arms helplessly in front and obliging her to lean forward at his mercy.

For a while he was content to sit alongside her, idly fondling her breasts as they hung heavily down, fingers circling her nipples, twisting and pulling until she gasped aloud, writhing helplessly. Smiling with quiet satisfaction, he let go of her breasts, passing his hands down her belly, probing between her parted thighs, feeling the warm wetness there. Her skin fluttered beneath his touch as he brushed ever so gently against the open and yearning lips of her sex, feeling those lips quivering in arousal.

"Wider."

In response to his whispered commands, trembling all the while under his touch, Julia moved her knees further and further apart. Her belly bowed down onto the sheet and her back arched into a gentle curve held in tension by the sash binding her wrists so that her sex was fully exposed and her buttocks jutted out sharply behind her.

Another slender leather strap was lifted from the bedpost and he moved to stand behind her. Julia tensed, her face flaming crimson at how openly and shamelessly she was displayed to him and her heart pounding at the thought of how easily and confidently he exercised his control over her. He paused, enjoying the sight of her so wantonly spread, the red stripes of the thrashing still plainly evident on the rounded flesh of her backside and in stark contrast to the pale tan of her thighs.

Thwack!
Thwack!

Slowly and deliberately he began to whip her thighs, relishing the way Julia gasped and squirmed right from the first stinging stroke.

Thwack!

Thwack!

Julia bucked and heaved, gasping and moaning aloud as the leather whipped relentlessly up the length of one smooth thigh and back down the other. She could feel each stroke searing her flesh, the pale skin reddening rapidly and the heat building and creeping towards the gaping slit of her sex.

Thwack!

Thwack!

Julia writhed under the onslaught, and yet the sharp sting of the strap combined with her submissive exposure inflamed her unwanted arousal, the lips of her sex swelling and opening wider between her widespread thighs. Suddenly she felt a surge of desire to be whipped there and jerked herself back, thrusting her belly higher to meet the strap. Her breathing quickened, the shocked gasps and cries of pain giving way to low moans of desire as she thrust her backside higher and higher.

Thwack!

Thwack!

Two final stinging strokes whipped in, setting her writhing and squirming even more urgently, and then the strap was tossed aside.

She almost sobbed with frustration. She understood only too well that her lover would amuse himself by bringing her repeatedly to the brink, taking his own pleasure as he wished but withholding from her the ultimate release until the time of his choosing. Drawing her thighs together, squeezing the wet and gaping lips of her sex would be enough now to bring about that release but she waited, as she must, passive and obedient to her lover.

Quickly he knelt alongside her, his hands slipping under her body and closing around her dangling breasts. Her nipples were hard and hot and she cried out at once, pressing her breasts down into his hands. He grunted with satisfaction and turned away, reaching this time for a slender cane.

Julia's gaze followed him, her eyes pleading even though she knew there was no hope of a respite. Her whole body was hot and quivering, glistening with a sheen of perspiration and the scent of her arousal hung heavy in the air. The merest brush of a cock or a hand between her thighs would be sufficient to trigger a shattering orgasm but she waited, helpless and obedient, Her lover flexed the cane, watching her reaction as she imagined it's sharp bite across her already flogged and tender flesh.

"Please ... no!"

Julia knew that pleas for mercy would fall on deaf ears but knew too that they were expected of her. Her pleas were not wholly groundless nor part of an act to please him. She hated the cane, hated its searing bite, and she shuddered at the thought of it being whipped hard and without mercy into her already seared flesh. Yet fearful as she was, she knew that it's sting would bring about the release she craved and she felt a perverse excitement throbbing inside her.

But he prolonged her awful anticipation, flexing the slender rod and snapping it sharply through the air before finally rising to his feet.

Brandishing the cane in front of her, he revelled in her helpless exposure, his erection swelling as he imagined her writhing and howling out loud, begging and pleading as he lashed her without mercy.

His hand encircled his cock, stroking the swelling length of flesh, working himself slowly harder and firmer.

"You want this rammed up inside you, don't you?"

"Yes, yes," she found herself pleading. "Oh yes!"

Her voice was husky, her eyes fixed longingly on the cock. Her tongue ran lightly around her lips and her jutting hips quivered.

"But first, you need a good dose of this!"

Julia clenched her buttocks as he laid the cane alongside his now fully erect cock, taunting and mocking her. He moved out of her sight, taking his place at the foot of the bed. Julia knew that she could turn her head, straining around to watch him, but she kept her gaze fixed firmly ahead, eyes focused on her bound wrists. Her breathing was slow and deep as she braced herself against the coming onslaught but she was unable to stifle a sharp gasp of trepidation as she felt the cane laid lightly across the still tingling globes of her backside.

Swish!
Whack!

The cane lifted and whipped back down in a shallow arc even as Julia tensed herself, the sharp smack of supple wood against pliant flesh ringing around the room. She reacted at once, her back arching and her hips squirming as the first stinging stripe cut into the already tender flesh of her bottom. From between her desperately clamped lips came a shocked gasp as the fiery heat bit into her.

Swish!
Thwack!
Swish!
Thwack!

Without waiting for her writhing to cease, he whipped in a second stinging stroke and then a third, shattering her flimsy resistance. Tears trickled from the corners of Julia's eyes and she howled out loud. Her whole being seemed centred on the throbbing cheeks of her backside, now cruelly striped with three thin and rapidly reddening welts, and her hips jerked wildly from side to side as though to both escape the torment and fan cooling air over the heated flesh.

Swish!
Whack!

Swish!

Whack!

Switching his aim, her lover whipped the cane up across Julia's most tender flesh where her buttocks curved gently into her thighs, spurring her to even more frenzied writhing and twisting. Julia was breathless, her body hot and drenched with sweat, the heat and pain of the thrashing gripping her backside and spreading rapidly into her belly.

Between her thighs she could feel a warm wetness and then a surge of lust washed over her, overlying the pain and shame of the beating and the submission. She was beyond coherent thought, trembling on the brink of release, her hips swinging and jerking to the rhythm of the thrashing.

Her breasts pressed down onto the bed, erect nipples rubbing against the satin sheets with each convulsive jerk of her hips and, despite herself, sending ripples of pleasure coursing through her belly as she thrust her bottom higher and higher to receive each new stroke.

She could take no more and her lover knew it.

Tossing the cane aside he knelt on the bed between her spread thighs. His cock was fully erect, aroused both by the act of thrashing her and the sight and sounds of her helpless struggles.

She was ready for him, her sex gaping and dripping wet, the musky scent of her exciting him further. Seizing her around the waist he turned her onto her back. The sash binding her wrists twisted easily and she whimpered as her bruised and battered buttocks bounced against the bed. He knelt above her, his cock along her belly, hands reaching eagerly for her tender breasts.

Julia cried out loud as his fingers closed around her nipples, wriggling beneath him as the first spasms of orgasm rippled through her. He knew she was coming and wasted no time, slipping down her body and entering her in one smooth thrust. The penetration triggered her waiting orgasm and she cried aloud again and again, shuddering beneath him as he thrust into her.

His hands left her breasts, slipping quickly down under her to grasp at her buttocks, lifting her clear of the bed. Julia cried out louder, his urgent grip on her stinging backside inflaming the pain of the thrashing and then a more powerful spasm swept through her belly. Wrapping her legs around her lover's waist she opened herself wider, dragging him deeper and deeper into the quivering pit of her sex, spasm after spasm racing through her belly and breasts as she came again and again.

Shuddering and trembling, a mist of sweat clouding her eyes, she felt her lover climax deep inside her, the hot spurts triggering yet another convulsive orgasm until at last she was spent and lay passive and trembling beneath him.

He lay heavily across her, hands lazily fondling her still hard and swollen nipples, and then he rolled aside, reaching up at last to untie her wrists.

Julia didn't stir. The exposure, the bondage, the thrashings and finally, the explosive orgasms that had racked her body had drained her completely and she slept, limp and exhausted.

fatigue, her nipples were hard and erect, and he couldn't resist reaching down, fingertips flicking across them.

"Come on now. No slacking."

His fingers flicked at her again, harder, the sharp contact drawing quick gasps from her as she hauled her arms straight.

"I can't... too heavy..."

"Make the twenty or you go back on the treadmill before you try again."

Julia shuddered and strained harder, finally succeeding in bringing the weights together again.

"Only four more."

Only! Gritting her teeth, Julia hauled her arms up. She was quivering all over with the effort, every muscle screaming. Ricky reached for her breasts once more, squeezing the firm mounds in both hands as she struggled to complete the task. Her nipples rubbed insistently against his palms and she could feel herself becoming aroused, her concentration slipping away. Desperately she sucked in her breath and made a supreme effort. The weights touched above her head, once, twice, three and finally, arms trembling, four times.

Limply she sagged back, uncaring of the drag on her arms and shoulders or of Ricky enthusiastically massaging her straining hard nippled breasts. She was sure she could take no more. All that was left was for Ricky to fuck her as she lay on the bench and she knew she did not have the will or the strength to resist. Marsha looked down at her, a smile of satisfaction on her lips.

"Exhausted?"

"Yes."

It was all Julia could do to whisper the reply, her breasts still heaving as she gasped for breath.

"Perhaps one more routine?"

"Oh, no... please... I can't."

of her belly advertised her ready availability and submission to anyone who desired her.

Not just anyone! Only those select few who were of value to Mr Nico.

As she thought of Nico she shivered and dropped her hands to her sides. The car would be waiting outside. She dressed quickly, in so far as she was permitted to dress, casting a last glance around to make sure she had left nothing behind before leaving and locking the door firmly behind her.

The usual limousine with heavily tinted windows to the rear was waiting at the kerb. It made her feel like a film star and she was amused at the curious glances from passers by as she climbed inside, all of them no doubt wondering who she was. She almost laughed aloud as she thought of their reactions if they knew the truth.

"Good morning, Miss Julia," leered George, the chauffeur. As he handed her into the car he took the usual nip at her bottom, which there was no way of avoiding. The touch of his clammy fingers on her wrist as he did so made her flesh creep, and she did not reply, just settled herself carefully, very mindful of her sore behind.

"Been whipped again have we?"

Still she said nothing, just sat up straight. She was used to this ordeal. At last he steered the car into the morning traffic, not before he had adjusted the mirror ostentatiously, licking his lips as he took her in. She moved to avoid his gaze, but he just moved the mirror again. Like all of Nico's employees, he was well aware of what she was made to do and knew that she was permitted nothing under the thin dress.

"Mr Nico is in a meeting all morning but he says he'll call later and do lunch."

He glanced quickly back at her to confirm she understood and turned his attention back to the traffic while Julia settled more comfortably into her seat. The fact that Nico was busy meant that she had the whole morning to herself, and she intended to make good use of the chance to relax. Nico had been very busy just lately and she hadn't seen his sister Natalie for weeks.

The thought of Natalie sent a tremor rippling through her, for Natalie had a dark, sadistic side to her nature. Julia both feared Natalie and yet felt strangely drawn towards her. The young woman never failed to unlock some deeply rooted desires within her.

So wrapped up was she in her thoughts that the car pulled up outside her apartment block without her realising she had arrived, and it took a few seconds and a discreet cough from George before she pulled herself together.

She swung her hips provocatively as she walked into the block, aware of his eyes on her every step of the way, revelling in the knowledge that however much he wanted her he could do nothing more than look.

Behind her, George licked his lips and shifted in his seat to ease the pressure on his crotch as he watched her out of sight. Then he floored the throttle, accelerating hard into the traffic to give some small relief to his frustrations.

Inside her apartment, Julia at once set the coffee percolator bubbling and nibbled on a croissant as she ran herself a hot bath, pouring a generous quantity of scented oil into the water.

She stripped off her clothes, waiting until the bath was almost half full, the scent of the oil hanging sweet and heavy in the air, before stepping in and lowering herself carefully down into the hot foam. The water explored every inch of her body, relaxing her at once, and she stretched sensuously, her bubble coated breasts breaking the surface like two tiny exotic islands.

Slowly and deliberately she ran her hands over and around the curves of her body, lying right back with her eyes half closed as the water warmed her. She was sensitive to her body's reactions, feeling each small tremor that ran through her as her hands stroked slowly down her belly, hesitating briefly before delving down between her parted thighs. The lips there were open already as if anticipating her touch, and she stroked slowly and carefully around them, feeling each small twitch as she gently caressed her most sensitive places.

No man ever took the time to pleasure her like this. All her 'lovers' ever wanted, if not to beat her - for to be allowed by Nico to do that was the main attraction - was to fondle her, usually roughly and seldom with any consideration for her feelings. Most were interested only in abusing or penetrating her, but always her wayward body responded.

Alone now, she took her time, feeling the heat and tension growing steadily inside her with each slow passage of her fingers around her sex. Her breasts bobbed above the surface of the water, bubbles sparkling on the smooth curves. They rose and fell gently in time with her steady breathing, the warm water lapping around them like a tide. She smiled to herself as she squinted down at them, imagining how inviting they would look to a watching lover.

None of them had ever been able to resist her breasts, fondling or mauling them repeatedly and she was certain her nipples had grown larger and become even more sensitive over the past few months.

She raised a hand to them now, brushing her finger tips lightly over the erect buds and sighing softly in response to the tremor that her touch provoked. Again and harder this time she caressed herself, feeling the tremors rippling down into her belly with every pass of her fingers.

She could feel her sex swelling and opening between her thighs, her fingers there slipping irresistibly deeper. Her clitoris throbbed urgently, demanding her attention. She abandoned her breasts, thrusting both hands impulsively down between her thighs. Her orgasm gripped her at once, the first sharp spasm stiffening her body and stifling her cries of pleasure. Her back arched as the tremors rippled out from her belly, slowly at first then faster and faster in time with the urgent thrusting of her fingers into the gaping slash of her sex until her whole body shook.

The water surged over her quivering breasts in warm waves and the room echoed to her gasps and moans. Her bruised and abused buttocks bounced against the bottom of the bath, the sharp stabbing pain spearing up into her sex and adding an extra dimension to the spasms racking her body.

"Ahhhhhh ... ahhhhhh."

One last spasm ripped through her and she fell back limply, body shuddering in the aftermath of her explosive release. She was totally relaxed now, all the tensions drained away and ready to face whatever the day had to offer.

The aroma of fresh coffee filtered through the door and she gave one last sigh of contentment before hauling herself upright and reaching for the towel.

Chapter Three

It was ten thirty and Julia relaxed by the window enjoying a late breakfast of coffee and croissants. She was dressed only in her bathrobe, her body still warmly scented and tingling deliciously in the afterglow of a very satisfying orgasm.

The view from her window never failed to fascinate and excite her, looking out as it did over the park in one of the most fashionable districts of the city, with the glittering towers of skyscrapers silhouetted along the skyline. The apartment itself was spacious, air conditioned and luxuriously furnished, in sharp contrast to the cramped and often damp bed sit she had left behind in England. It was all she had been able to afford on her student grant and the money she had earned as a part time barmaid and she had hated it.

Not even a year ago.

How trusting and naive she had been then, stupid even. Stupid enough to trust Martin, a man she had thought of then as her first real lover. A seemingly wealthy and undeniably attractive man who had held out to her the promise of a more exciting life. A man who had tricked her into smuggling drugs which were the real source of his wealth and who had abandoned her without a second thought when things went badly wrong in Central America.

She shuddered as she remembered her panic at being arrested, her desperate but futile attempt at escape, and the humiliation that had followed her recapture when she had been beaten and thrown naked into a police cell. The certainty of a long prison sentence had filled her with dread and then like a lifeline, she had been offered an alternative. Not a pleasant alternative, far from it, but she was in a poor bargaining position.

Serve three months in a corrective centre for prostitutes and petty thieves and she could walk free. She understood that to accept would mean submitting herself to a harsh regime of hard work, frequent beatings and obedience to her guards but she had little choice.

She had signed the necessary papers and in that harsh regime she had discovered a dark and barely suspected side to her sexuality.

At the hands of her young male guards her sexual experience was ruthlessly and even brutally broadened and yet far from filling her with fear and shame, the humiliating submission and the frequent beatings she was made to endure served only to excite and arouse her. Part way through her three month term and because of her strange reaction to the harsh treatment, she was sent to work at the house of Mr Nico and his sister Natalie. There, her sexuality was fully exploited both for their own entertainment and more especially for that of their many guests and she had responded fully, almost eagerly to their every whim and desire until the day came when her sentence was complete.

She had an airline ticket back to England and her former life and then Nico had offered her a job, this job, and she had accepted. He wanted her to entertain his contacts in New York just as she had done at his house but now she would be well paid for her efforts. Even now her acceptance surprised her but she knew that the alternative of returning to England to pick up the strands of her life was not a prospect that filled her with joy.

Nico worked her hard, her diary seemingly full of appointments with rich and influential men, and sometimes women, who wanted nothing more than to use and abuse her for their own pleasure. Nothing surprised her any more.

However bizarre the demands of her 'lovers', she accommodated them all, even taking a perverse pleasure in her situation.

She occasionally found herself gazing wistfully in the direction of attractive young men in the street, imagining how they would be between the sheets. It was impossible of course, for Nico demanded she be available twenty four hours a day and she had no time for anything like a normal date. In any case, the young man she selected might not be able to bring her to orgasm - it took a severe beating to do that!

If she was living her life in a cage, at least it was a very well gilded cage and she wasn't about to complain too loudly.

She glanced at the clock on the wall, startled to notice that an hour had slipped by while she was lost in her thoughts. George would be bringing the car for her soon to have lunch with Nico. She wasn't sure about after that but then again she wasn't paid to do anything other than obey and she was very good at that.

Very good indeed.

Chapter Four

Nico had booked a table at a smart new bistro and Julia was really looking forward to the lunch. George deliberately dropped her some way from the door and watched her as she walked erotically to the door, trying to control her high heels and short skirt in the blustery weather.

The interior was dark after the bright sunshine outside and the place seemed crowded and noisy as she peered around for Nico. He saw her first, waving her over to a table near the bar and as she threaded her way across the room she saw that Natalie was with him. Julia's heart skipped a beat for Natalie had been out of town for a few weeks and would no doubt be looking forward to renewing her relationship with her. She licked her lips at the thought, mentally reviewing her diary and not altogether surprised to discover that she had been left free for the rest of the week.

"Good afternoon, Julia."

Nico rose politely, pulling out a chair for her, and Julia nodded her own greetings, her heart beating a little faster as Natalie smiled at her.

"You're looking good, Julia," said Natalie. "The work must suit you."

She blushed slightly, still a little embarrassed to have the 'work' she did for Nico actually mentioned aloud. Natalie leaned across to her.

"After we finish here we'll go shopping together."

Julia buried her nose in the menu to cover her blushes, knowing very well how the shopping trip would end and knowing that Nico knew too. The bistro was busy but Nico seemed to have some influence with the management for they were served very quickly and as soon as the waiters withdrew he got down to business.

"Do you follow politics much, Julia?"

"No, hardly at all really. I know there was an election a while ago but that's about all."

Nico scowled and Julia wondered if she should have been taking a greater interest but he hastened to reassure her.

"Yeah, that damned election cost me a lot of good contacts, and now there's talk of a crusade to stamp out corruption in government."

"Don't all governments talk like that?"

"Oh, sure, but this administration means it. I lost two good guys in the justice department last week. Resignations due to ill health before they got hauled up in front of a board of enquiry."

"I see."

Perhaps that was why her diary was suddenly less full than usual. Natalie joined the conversation, leaning across the table to be sure of not being overheard.

"The thing is, we need to establish some new contacts in key positions." Nico grinned and stuffed a forkful of pasta into his mouth. "So you are going to be worked much harder in future!"

"Oh."

Julia felt a little confused but Natalie hastened to explain.

"Thing is, Julia, every barrel has a few rotten apples and once we find them..."

"You're up and running again?"

"That's right."

Nico regarded her carefully as Julia considered her position.

"What about the current crop of rotten apples?"

"The current crop! Hey, that's funny."

Nico pondered the question for a few moments.

"I guess we'll have to keep a few on just in case they get re-elected next time around and a couple of others know too much but otherwise they've outlived their usefulness."

"What my dear brother is getting round to is, you have to be even more - er - co-operative to our friends than before. The whole thing has got harder for us, and that means harder for you, right?"

Julia thought about it for a few minutes.

"I don't suppose some of them would just settle for a bit more - er - straight -"

"Oh no! Sex is such a universal currency and your particular exchange rate is very favourable."

Nico grinned at his own joke and Julia thought about it again. She was horrified at the thought of being introduced to a whole crowd of new 'lovers' with their new and probably obscene demands, but there was also an undeniable tingle of excitement in her belly at the prospect. After all, she reasoned, it could be no worse than her experiences on first starting to work for Nico or come to that, the first few weeks of her brief stay in prison.

"I've got no choice, have I?" she said reluctantly.

Nico beamed with satisfaction. He had enjoyed tormenting her a little in public. Then his smile darkened to a scowl.

"Who let him in here?"

Julia followed his gaze and saw a young well dressed man entering the bistro in company with a somewhat tartily dressed young woman. The man was followed by a number of obvious minders, and Julia guessed that he was in some degree at least, one of Nico's competitors. He saw Nico at once and headed across to the table, narrowly beating the suddenly anxious looking head waiter.

"Hi, Nico, how you doin'?"

He thrust out a hand and Nico took it grudgingly.

"Fine, Carlos, just fine."

Now that the man was closer Julia could see that he shared the same Latin origins as Nico, but whereas Nico was starting to run to fat, Carlos obviously kept himself in shape. He exuded an air of confidence which somehow impressed her despite Nico's surly and dismissive manner towards him, and there was something else, something she couldn't quite define but which caught her attention as she studied him discreetly.

"I told my friends we'd be sure to meet some interesting folks here and I was right."

Carlos acknowledged Natalie with a brief nod and turned his attention to Julia, subjecting her to a long scrutiny.

"Who's the good looking broad, Nico ? I don't remember seeing her before."

Nico made the introductions and Carlos immediately became interested.

"So! I've never met you but I've sure heard plenty."

He looked her up and down again, undressing her with his eyes, and Julia fidgeted nervously in her chair.

"Say, Nico, how about Julia and me?"

"Not a chance, Carlos, unless you're in a position to do me some real heavy favours of course."

"I've got a few contacts in the new administration could be useful."

Nico laughed out loud.

"Sure you have, Carlos. A few file clerks and secretaries!"

"Better than that. You know, Nico, I think maybe we should get together and really clean up."

Nico laughed again although his expression was far from friendly.

"I don't need you to be big time, Carlos - and all you want is a free poke at Julia."

The other man flushed at the insult.

"If that's the way you want to play that's fine by me but don't expect any favours."

He submitted Julia to another keen scrutiny.

"Too bad, honey, your owner won't let you play right now but I'll see what I can do."

He leered lecherously at her, showing lots of white teeth and then nodded to them all.

"Enjoy your lunch, folks."

Nico watched sourly as the head waiter showed Carlos and his party to a table at the far side of the room.

"Standards are slipping all over these days."

Julia could feel her heart beating a little faster, her face still flushed from the way Carlos had looked at her.

"Who was that?"

"Carlos ? He worked for me a few years ago then got high and mighty ideas about branching out on his own."

He grimaced and Julia got the impression that the parting had been far from friendly.

"Anyway, he's strictly small time although he works hard at pretending otherwise."

Natalie leaned forward, glancing in the direction of Carlos' table.

"Maybe he does have some useful connections?"

"No way. Like I said, he's small time. Probably screwing a secretary somewhere."

Nico seemed to cheer up at the thought and turned his full attention back to Julia.

"As I was saying, Natalie is working on a number of likely prospects so be prepared to do your stuff any time in the next few weeks."

Julia nodded, the excitement tingling inside her again.

"In the meantime, both me and Natalie will be very busy so to save you checking with us I'm going to tell Natalie to let our new prospects know that they can have a free hand with you."

Julia felt her heart skip a couple of beats and her mouth went dry. She understood very well what that meant. It meant that instead of her lovers being divided into two groups of those allowed merely to fuck her and the more privileged, who were additionally allowed to whip her, she would be required to submit herself fully to the whims of whoever laid claim to her. That she would be whipped more often she had no doubt for she was all too aware of the erotic excitement it generated in others to see her writhing under the lash.

She felt the excitement churning stronger in her belly even though she was anxious about whatever lay ahead. She knew that Nico vetted those allowed access to her very strictly and always let her know their preferences in advance but now that safeguard seemed to be getting swept away. At the same time she found the thought of not knowing exactly what lay in store for her from the new lovers strangely enticing and her belly churned again.

Nico sat back satisfied and Natalie's foot reached under the table to press against Julia's. Julia felt suddenly heady and breathless, aware that she was facing harder tests than before. She picked up her wine glass, noticing without surprise the trembling in her fingers.

"We'll finish up here," said Natalie, "and then go shopping."

There was a gleam in her eye that promised much more than shopping. As Natalie's foot pressed once more up against her own, Julia felt a surge of desire rising up inside her. On the other side of the room, loud laughter rang out from Carlos' party and as she glanced across she saw Carlos looking directly at her. Unseen by either Nico or Natalie, he raised his arm in the unmistakable gesture of sex and despite herself she felt a jolt of dread in the pit of her stomach.

Chapter Five

As Julia followed Natalie from the bistro, she glanced once more towards Carlos' table. He was watching her again, making no secret of his interest and she felt a frisson of excitement at the thought of submitting herself to his desires. He obviously knew a lot about her and probably wouldn't hesitate to give full rein to his darker desires. The thought sent another shiver of fear through her and she had to remind herself that Nico would never agree to lending her to Carlos, however briefly. For now, she had Natalie to deal with and there was no mistaking the fact that the young girl was excited about something other than a mere shopping expedition. Certainly there was no doubt that she would end the afternoon by pleasuring Natalie and she was certain that Natalie would show her cruel side.

But, Julia felt, there was something else in store, something that she could not avoid, something that filled her with foreboding.

As the lunch had progressed, Natalie had became more and more animated, constantly pressing her foot against Julia's and eventually slipping off her shoe altogether and running her foot up the length of Julia's legs under the concealment of the table cloth.

Nico, while fully aware of what was going on right alongside him, concentrated on his meal although even he had permitted himself a small knowing smile whenever he looked at her. Now, following Natalie to the car waiting for them outside, she felt the young girl's excitement rising still more and a tingle of anticipation ran through her own body.

As she had expected, the car was a limousine with darkened glass to the rear windows. Nico and Natalie rarely travelled in anything else and by now Julia was well aware that the darkened windows served a deeper purpose than merely concealing the identity of the occupants. On more than one occasion, while accompanying Nico to and from some meeting or other, she had been told to bend across his lap and suck him off.

Several times, after a concluding a particularly successful deal, Nico had stripped her naked and fucked her on the leather seats, her cries muffled by the heavy doors and thick glass as the car weaved through rush hour traffic.

It came as no surprise therefore, that even as she settled herself into her seat, Natalie turned to her, eyes shining.

"Open your blouse! Quickly!"

Her lips were wet and parted, her voice low and husky with an excitement that transmitted itself to Julia as she reached for the buttons. Her fingers shook but one by one they came loose and she pulled the blouse free of her skirt. Her bra-less breasts spilled free, nipples already half erect and she began to slip the blouse from her shoulders.

"No, don't take it off..."

Julia sat still as Natalie reached out to trail her fingers softly around the proud swell of her breasts. She could feel her heart beating faster, her nipples becoming firmer as Natalie's fingers brushed across them.

"Good. Very good. Make them really hard for me."

With only the slightest hesitation, Julia did as she was told. She was well trained now. She lifted her hands and began to caress herself, slowly at first, her fingers circling tantalisingly around her nipples.

Natalie watched intently, licking her lips as Julia's nipples swelled and hardened, darkening rapidly to a deep red in contrast to the pale tan of her breasts. Julia's hands were moving faster now, small shocks jolting her breasts with each pass across her tender buds. She grasped them between her finger and thumb, teasing them out from her body, gasping out loud at the shocks rippling through her. She could feel how hard they were, jutting like fat ripe berries from her breasts. Between her thighs her body responded, warm wetness bathing her sex, and she wondered if Natalie intended to make her come.

"Are they hot and hard?"

"Yes, oh yes, so hard..."

Julia could barely gasp out her reply but Natalie nodded.

"Then stop."

"Ohhhhh."

A shudder of disappointment ran through Julia's body but she dropped her hands at once and sat facing Natalie, her breasts heaving and her face flushed. Natalie was holding something in her hands and she held it up so that Julia could see it. It was a gold ring, smaller than a normal ring but quite thick and heavy looking. Natalie was holding it up by two stubby tabs set into the bottom. As Julia watched, she squeezed the tabs together and the ring opened at the top. At once Julia guessed its purpose and she couldn't help but glance down at her engorged breasts before dragging her eyes back to the ring.

Surely there was no way it would fit!

She cringed back involuntarily but Natalie shook her head sternly. Sitting up straight, her heart pounding, she watched as Natalie reached out for her bare breast, fingers closing around the hard throbbing bud of her aroused nipple. She was held fast and sat as still as she could, holding her breath as Natalie slipped the open end of the ring over the distended bud.

The first ring snapped shut with a barely audible click. The pain was exquisite but brief. The second ring was attached at once and Natalie sat back to admire the effect while Julia struggled with her feelings. The rings fitted tightly and were certainly uncomfortable but at the same time she was aware of a heightened sensitivity in her breasts. Her nipples still throbbed and tingled but now the feeling was deeper, more intense. She turned slightly on the seat and her breasts swayed, the movement triggering a sharp spasm through her trapped flesh.

"You can fasten your blouse now."

With trembling fingers Julia buttoned her blouse, sucking her breath in sharply as the fabric brushed across her nipples and triggered yet more small spasms in her breasts. The feeling was initially painful, followed almost at once by a rush of pleasure.

Chapter Six

After two hours of shopping, Julia was in torment. The nipple rings felt like burning bands clamped around her swollen buds and each brush of her breasts against the fabric of her blouse sent a spasm lancing through her. It was a sensation quite unlike anything she had experienced before, a nagging, throbbing pain overlaid with a tingle of pleasure that served to keep her in a state of arousal throughout the afternoon.

Several times when she moved carelessly or turned sharply, she had been forced to suck in her breath and shut her eyes as the sudden spasm gripped her. On more than one occasion the shop assistants had been moved to enquire if she felt faint so extreme had been her reaction.

Natalie made her try on a seemingly endless selection of blouses, watching in amusement as Julia gingerly eased her way into each new garment. After a while she had insisted that they visit the lingerie department, picking out a choice of bras for Julia to try, though normally they were forbidden her. The stabbing pains that gripped her breasts as she fastened each new bra in place and modelled it for Natalie took her breath away and brought tears to her eyes, but still her body remained physically aroused.

Her legs trembled and she could feel the wet and parted lips of her sex rubbing urgently against the crotch of her panties with each step she took. She wondered if anyone else apart from Natalie was aware of her aroused state and what their reaction would be if they knew the cause.

"Look at yourself."

Natalie's voice was husky with barely suppressed excitement and Julia turned to stare at her reflection in the changing room mirror. She was stripped to the waist, her slender, stocking sheathed legs and short skirt serving only to emphasise her partial nakedness. But her attention was held by her breasts. Heavy and swollen, they jutted out proudly from her body, her nipples straining out from their confining golden rings.

Never before had she seen her nipples so prominent or so red, swollen so large and hard that they seemed in danger of bursting like ripe succulent berries. Without conscious thought she lifted her hands, fingers hovering in front of her body, wondering what it would feel like to be fondled or kissed on those straining buds and how her body would react to the sensations such a caress would unleash.

"Are they sore?"

"I - I don't know."

It was amazing, but now that she was looking at herself so openly she was unsure what she could feel. Sensitive yes, and certainly very tender, but the sensation of pain that had nagged at her nerve endings all afternoon seemed to melt away in a rush of pure pleasure as her fingers brushed up against her imprisoned flesh.

Natalie grinned, stepping up behind her and reaching round to push her fingers aside.

"Not just yet. I may want to shop here again."

She laughed softly and Julia took a deep breath, fighting her wayward feelings back under some semblance of control before bending to pick up her blouse.

"Time to go, I think."

Natalie looked at her watch and Julia felt a thrill of - excitement? Fear? It was strange, knowing that she was a slave to this sadistic young woman, and being unable to resist the perverse thrill that knowledge worked upon her unwilling flesh.

Natalie kept quiet on the subject of what she had planned for the remainder of the afternoon and Julia spent the short trip from the city centre in an agony of suspense, her emotions heightened by the feel of the rings still firmly clamped around her nipples.

Shopping for the clothes and perfumes that were stowed safely in the back of the car they had been like two close friends but she knew that once inside Natalie's apartment their relationship would shift to Mistress and slave and she would experience extremes of pain and pleasure at the hands of the young girl sitting beside her until both of them were utterly exhausted. The prospect both scared and fascinated her and she felt her stomach twisting into a hard knot of anticipation as the car drew up outside the building.

Natalie wasted no time, hurrying ahead to summon an elevator while Julia and the driver divided the shopping between them and struggled along behind.

"Thank you, Lee. Take the rest of the afternoon off and be back here to collect us at nine thirty."

"Sure thing, Miss Natalie."

Lee smirked knowingly at Julia while Julia herself gave Natalie a questioning glance.

"Collect us?"

Natalie punched the button for the penthouse and the lift doors hissed shut.

"I have to catch a plane back to California tonight. I'll explain later, but it's all to do with what we discussed at lunch."

Julia guessed that Natalie would tell her no more than bare essentials anyway and stopped wondering. Far more important right now was how Natalie intended to pass the time until nine thirty and she would be finding that out very soon.

Chapter Seven

"I think it's time we made ourselves more comfortable and took off our clothes, Julia."

Julia nodded wordlessly and replaced her wine glass on the low table in front of her before standing up to face Natalie. She had expected to be told to strip at once but Natalie had deliberately prolonged her suspense by insisting that they have a glass of wine and a light snack while watching the late afternoon news on TV and for Julia the time had crawled by. Her stomach was knotted into a tight ball and she could feel her mouth suddenly dry as Natalie too rose to her feet.

"Together I think."

Natalie was already unbuttoning her blouse and Julia nodded, her fingers shaking as she fumbled over the first few buttons. Unlike Julia, Natalie wore a bra beneath her blouse, a wispy froth of white silk and lace which held but barely concealed the firm swell of her breasts. Her nipples were already erect, dark circles thrusting prominently against the tautly stretched silk. She dropped her hands to the waistband of her skirt, nodding to Julia to do the same and seconds later the two garments rustled softly to the floor. Another brief nod and Julia's fingers were busy at her suspenders, unclipping her sheer stockings and peeling them down her legs. The suspender belt was next, unhooked and tossed aside, leaving her totally naked, for she was not allowed panties.

For the moment, Natalie remained dressed in her lingerie, emphasising the fact that she was in control. Julia licked her lips nervously, aware that whatever ordeal Natalie had planned for her would not properly begin until the young girl was totally naked too.

"Shall I remove those rings?"

Julia hesitated, wary of some trap but the question demanded an answer.

"Please, Mistress."

She didn't really expect a positive response and was taken by surprise as Natalie reached out for her.

"Well, I suppose enough is enough for the first time."

Her fingers closed delicately around the tabs on each ring, squeezing them fully open and Julia could barely restrain a gasp as her tender flesh tingled from the sudden release of so many hours of unrelenting pressure.

"There now, no damage done."

This time Julia could not suppress a low moan as Natalie ran her fingers lightly around the still throbbing buds, short, sharp shocks darting through her breasts in time with the beating of her heart.

"They turned you on, didn't they?"

Julia moaned as Natalie trailed her fingers down her belly, knowing what she would find.

"Yes, you're all hot and wet."

Natalie's eyes glinted in triumph as she burrowed between Julia's thighs, watching the conflicting emotions her activities were arousing. Julia's legs trembled and her bare breasts heaved as she felt her self control slipping away.

"Please, Mistress, please..."

Her whole body was alive with arousal, her breathing quick and ragged under the persistent stimulation. She wanted Natalie's fingers inside her, thrusting deep, opening her wider and wider until her orgasm engulfed her.

"Not yet." Natalie stepped back a pace and Julia sagged, almost falling forward. Frustration and shame at how easily she had allowed herself to be manipulated flooded through her in equal measure as she forced herself to stand upright.

"I want you face down on the bed."

In a moment, Natalie had become the dominating mistress and Julia hurried to obey, stretching out full length on top of the king sized bed. She couldn't see Natalie now unless she twisted round to look but was aware of her entering the bedroom behind her a few minutes later.

"Push yourself up a little."

Again Julia obeyed without question, pushing her breasts and belly clear of the bed as Natalie knelt alongside her. She could feel the heavy leather of a strap brushing against her flanks and tensed, expecting to be beaten, but instead Natalie laid the belt she was holding on the bed beneath her.

"Lie down again."

The belt was fastened around her waist and buckled down hard across the small of her back and without waiting to be told she offered up her arms.

"Good girl."

Natalie took her wrists and passed them through two loops stitched into the belt, pulling them tight and binding her arms behind her. She expected to be told to turn over to present Natalie with her defenceless belly and breasts and began to wriggle in preparation.

"No, I'm not finished yet."

Natalie slid from the bed and Julia felt her ankles seized, a leather strap buckled tight around first one and then the other.

"Bend your legs ... right up ..."

Suiting her actions to her words, Natalie seized Julia's legs, bending them fully back until her ankles touched her buttocks. Now she could feel two short chains dangling from the straps around her ankles and guessed at once that her feet too were to be fastened alongside her wrists. Another pull at her legs and then two sharp clicks sounded behind her leaving her trussed and totally helpless. The leather belt around her waist cinched tight while the chains fastening her ankles to it pulled her body into a shallow arc. To add to her discomfort and apprehension, her ankles had been clipped to each side of her waist dragging her thighs well apart and leaving her belly and sex fully exposed.

Apart from twisting from side to side there was no way she could move and now Natalie rolled her over onto her back. Julia knew that Natalie loved to see her naked and bound, waiting helpless and tense to satisfy her desires. The sight excited and aroused her, tingles of pleasure could be seen rippling through her as she thought of what she could do to Julia.

Natalie smiled as Julia lay in front of her, shoulders flat to the bed but with her belly upthrust and her thighs apart as though inviting penetration. She looked warily up at Natalie, aware of how vulnerable she now was and very apprehensive about what was to come. Natalie was animated, her lips parted and wet, her eyes gleaming. She too had now stripped totally naked and her breasts swung forward as she bent to pick something up from the floor.

Something... there was no doubt at all in Julia's mind that it would be some kind of whip, and she waited dry mouthed and anxious to see just what Natalie had selected.

"What do you think?"

Natalie's voice was breathless with excitement as she held up the whip for Julia to see, and Julia could barely repress a shudder as she gazed up at it. Instead of the usual many thonged instrument she had become accustomed to Natalie using on her, this whip was a short thong of heavily braided leather, the tip splayed out wide and flat.

There was no doubt that the sting it delivered would be most excruciating in the right hands and she knew from experience that Natalie was an expert when it came to whips of any sort. She licked her lips nervously, her eyes darting between the whip and Natalie as the young girl turned it this way and that.

"Yes, Julia, I'm sure it will really sting but that's not the best bit! Look!"

She shifted her grip, allowing the hand grip to dangle down, and now Julia could see that it was fashioned into the shape of an erect penis, about seven or eight inches long and quite thick. Her eyes widened and Natalie smiled down at her reaction.

"Recognise it, do you?"

Despite her sudden shock, Julia managed to nod as Natalie dangled the instrument even closer, her smile becoming more wicked.

"Of course you do. Nico had the cast taken just for you and says you should think of him whenever you use it - or rather, whenever it gets used on you."

She laughed out loud at her little joke and Julia shuddered again as Natalie swung the handle up between her parted thighs to smack gently against her sex. To her acute embarrassment she felt herself reacting to the touch, her sex lips twitching involuntarily and she hoped Natalie hadn't noticed.

"Now there are no prizes for guessing where this is going but first there's another little matter to attend to."

Reversing her grip, Natalie took a firm hold on the handle once more, flexing her wrist as she moved into position directly in front of Julia's bound and offered body.

"Are you ready for this?"

"Yes."

Julia barely breathed her reply as she braced herself against the coming onslaught. She wanted to close her eyes but knew that Natalie would only order her to keep them open - and besides, the whip commanded her undivided attention as Natalie drew back her arm.

Swish! Thwack!

The thong whistled through the air in a short arc and smacked down hard across the tender skin of Julia's inner thigh. She cried out at once at the stinging impact, her body heaving and twisting as a broad red welt deepened across her pale skin.

Swish! Thwack!

Barely giving her time to recover, Natalie whipped the strap in again, higher this time where Julia's flesh was even softer and more tender. Again she writhed under the searing slash, crying out loud in anguish as tears trickled from her eyes. Two strokes only and already her flesh was hot and stinging. She looked up at Natalie, her vision blurred by her tears, but saw no mercy in the intent face. Already she was drawing back her arm and Julia cringed back, biting her lip against the onslaught.

Swish! Crack!

Swish! Whack!

Two strokes delivered in rapid succession sent Julia squirming desperately across the bed, her bare breasts heaving as her hips shuddered and shook in response to the fierce bite of leather across her tender flesh.

Swish! Thwack!

Swish! Crack!

There was no escape as Natalie pursued her, the lash cracking down with an almost savage ferocity between her spread thighs. Natalie was elated, her own body alive with excitement as she watched the effect the thrashing was having on her helpless victim. Each crack of leather across Julia's offered thighs seemed to spur her to a higher plane of arousal and effort.

Julia writhed and squirmed in a vain attempt to avoid the stinging blows, crying out loud at every stroke, her cries dying slowly away to soft whimpers of pain as the welts striping her inner thighs deepened to a dark, throbbing redness.

Swish! Whack!

Swish! Crack!

The thong whipped in again, stinging her right up her thighs, almost smacking across the lips of her sex. She cried out even louder in a confusion of pain and dread, knowing exactly where Natalie intended to lay the next two strokes. There was nothing she could do to avoid them and she sucked in a deep breath, tensing every muscle in her belly and thighs against the expected pain.

As if in response, and maybe because she was so vulnerable, she suddenly felt a wave of arousal rising up inside her belly, her sex lips throbbing and swelling as though begging to be beaten. She whimpered anxiously, blinking back her tears as Natalie raised the whip again.

Swish! Crack!

With unerring accuracy Natalie laid the whip straight up between her thighs, the splayed and flattened tip smacking full across the open lips of her sex.

Julia howled.

Her body bucked as the fierce heat of the thrashing bit deep into her, the lips of her sex contracting back on themselves before swelling and darkening rapidly as the leather fell away and hot blood flooded into her abused flesh. The exquisite feeling of arousal swept away the pain and she gasped in response, feeling her sex peeling wetly open between her thighs, the lips throbbing steadily.

"Got to you at last!"

Natalie grinned wickedly, her hand slipping down between her own thighs, where she too was wet and open.

Swish! Thwack!

Again the broad tip of the thong smacked full against Julia's unprotected sex. This time, though she still howled in anguish at the sudden searing pain, she also shuddered with a strange delight as the pain fuelled her mounting arousal. A fine mist of droplets sprayed out onto her thighs, and when the lash fell away the tip was wet with her freely flowing juices.

The lips of her sex gaped redly, pulsating in response to both the sharp sting of the whip and the fierce passions that now gripped her. She pushed her shoulders back against the bed, thrusting her hips higher, offering herself shamelessly to the lash. Her cries gave way to soft whimpers of need and desire.

Natalie was possessed by desire too, her nipples hard and tingling, her own sex wet and open as she gazed down at her bound and helpless victim. Natalie's whole body was hot and trembling as she hurled herself onto the bed. Quickly and without ceremony she straddled Julia's body, her breasts swaying forward to brush against Julia's upthrust belly, her hips thrust back towards her face.

"Suck me, you bitch! Make me come!"

She pushed down harder and Julia strained upwards, her lips already parted and wet. She squirmed as her breasts were crushed softly beneath Natalie's body and then her questing mouth closed around the young girl's dripping slit. Natalie shuddered at once, arching her back to press down even harder against Julia's lips.

"Yes, yes, yes! Get your tongue in there!"

Natalie was panting with desire, her body rocking back and forth as the touch of Julia's eager lips and tongue sent sharp spasms of pleasure rippling through her. Julia's sex lips gaped wide open and wet, blood red and swollen from the thrashing. A wicked smile spread quickly across Natalie's face. Shifting her grip on the whip she still held tight, she leaned forward, centring the phallic handle between Julia's parted thighs.

"Come on, bitch, suck me... harder..."

With one smooth movement she pushed back and at the

same moment, thrust the handle of the whip deep into Julia's sex. Julia gasped at the sudden penetration, her hot breath funnelling up into Natalie's belly in an Ahhhhh of desire.

Natalie quivered all over, withdrawing the shaft and plunging it deep inside once more, her action rewarded by another gasp from Julia.

Natalie's actions were rhythmic now, her wrist pumping in and out as she reamed Julia's sex with the thick dildo, while her hips ground relentlessly down on her busy mouth. Julia herself was lost in a mindless daze, her body hot and perspiring, her mouth full of the aroma and taste of Natalie's rapidly approaching orgasm, while her own climax threatened to overwhelm her in a relentless tide of passion. Desperately she speared her tongue deep inside Natalie's slit, sucking and licking around the pulsating folds of flesh as she felt her self control ebbing away.

Julia's whole being seemed focused on the thick shaft pounding between her thighs, her actions becoming confused and disjointed. A flood of warm wetness bathed her face and she realised Natalie was climaxing, her body held taut and quivering, her wrist stilled as she held the dildo jammed deep inside Julia's belly.

Julia speared her tongue deeper, feeling the quivering growing into long spasms, slow at first then faster and faster until Natalie's whole body was shaking and shuddering above her. Her arms shook, driving the dildo deeper into Julia's sex and as Julia arched her back and thrust her hips forward her own orgasm claimed her. Gasping and moaning, her body racked by seemingly endless tremors of release she writhed beneath her mistress, dimly aware of Natalie writhing too, but otherwise lost in her own cocoon of pleasure until at last her body could take no more and she lay trembling and gasping.

Natalie too was spent, rolling over to lie panting alongside her, the dildo still glistening with the evidence of her orgasm slipping gradually free from Julia's sex.

Exhausted, both girls dozed for a while then Natalie roused Julia and unfastened her, lying back on the bed while Julia knelt between her thighs to pleasure her once more. Afterwards they bathed together, sharing the extra large bath while Natalie explained in a little more detail what she and Nico had already outlined and why it was necessary for her to return to California so soon.

"People in the new administration are out to make a name for themselves and I guess Nico and me are easy targets."

Julia nodded, stretching lazily in the warm, scented water as she listened. Politics didn't interest her at all but she understood what Natalie was telling her and how important it was for Nico to have friends in high places.

"So, until we can be sure our backs are covered we need to keep a low profile and it's better if we leave town for a few days."

Julia nodded again although she wished Natalie would get to the part that concerned her.

"You of course have to stay here. I've made a few promising contacts and they will be getting in touch over the next few days."

"They'll be contacting me direct?"

This was a new development.

"Yes. Some of them may be a little more difficult to deal with than the ones you've been used to. What they are doing for Nico is more important, so what they do to you doesn't matter, just remember that!"

Chapter Eight

For a whole week Julia heard nothing. Natalie and Nico were totally unavailable. Every morning she scanned the post and each time the telephone rang she felt her heart miss a beat, hurrying to answer the call and almost snatching at the handset in her eagerness. At last and when she least expected it, the call came late one afternoon, the businesslike manner of the caller sending waves of relief flooding through her as she listened to her brief instructions.

"Do you know the Regency Hotel?"

"Yes."

"Be there tonight at eight fifteen sharp, speak to no-one and go straight up to room eight fifteen."

"Room eight fifteen at eight fifteen, understood."

"Take the stairs. Not the lift."

"Stairs. Understood."

The line went dead and Julia stood for a few moments just staring at the receiver. Obviously she was not to be allowed any opportunity to find out in advance what lay in store for her, being required merely to place herself wholly at the disposal of whoever had summoned her without question or hesitation.

It had been a woman's voice, but that in itself told her very little. She wondered about it for a few moments, knowing from experience that the treatment she could expect from a woman would be very different from whatever she could expect from a man.

Whatever lay ahead she would find out soon enough and there was little time to spare. Apart from the timing, which left her only a little more than two hours to prepare and make her way to the hotel, the most pressing question was what to wear. She thought hard as she soaked in a hot bath, anxious to create a good impression.

Her apprehension was so intense that she was physically aroused, her nipples jutting firmly out from her breasts as she luxuriated in the hot scented water and she had to struggle hard to resist the urge to masturbate as her mind kept drifting off to wicked thoughts of what might lie ahead for her and only the knowledge that time was short gave her the resolve to climb out of the bath.

As she would be going into a public place and did not wish to attract undue attention, she had decided on a short but sensible skirt together with a silk blouse. Underwear was usually banned, but surely this was different? She settled on dark stockings and suspenders and a pair of brief, lace panties, so sheer that they clung to her like a second skin and revealed the shadowy outlines of her sex.

Her nipples were still swollen and erect and thrust proudly against the blouse, drawing attention to her breasts and openly advertising her arousal, so after a few moments thought she stripped it off and put on the matching lace bra to her panties, deciding that, initially at least, she should attempt some display of modesty.

It was dark by the time a cab dropped her in front of the hotel with just ten minutes to spare. She took a deep breath to compose herself before pushing through the revolving doors and striding across the lobby with a good deal more confidence than she felt, sure that she was being observed but forcing herself to look straight ahead.

Eight flights of stairs were more than she had tackled for a long time and she arrived at the eighth floor feeling short of breath and flustered, anxious now about being late, but room eight one five was just a few yards along the corridor and she had time to stand, drawing deep breaths and bringing her heartbeat back under control.

She was suddenly very nervous and even though her breathing was even and regular she was aware of her heart pounding loudly as she raised her hand to knock on the door, the time by her watch exactly a quarter past eight.

"Come in."

A man's voice, so the caller had probably been a secretary after all. Julia grasped the handle firmly, and then the door was open and she stepped forward. The room was dark, lit only by the light spilling through from the corridor, and as the door swung to behind her and full darkness returned, a bank of bright spotlights snapped on, illuminating a low stool set at the foot of the king size double bed.

"Stand in front of the stool with your back to the bed."

Without question, Julia walked across the room and took up position as ordered, the spotlights dazzling in her eyes as she strained to make out whoever was in the room with her. There were three shapes that she could dimly make out seated behind the bank of lights, but she was otherwise unable to make out any degree of detail although she had no doubt that she was clearly visible to them.

"You are Julia."

"Yes."

It had been a statement rather than a question but Julia felt compelled to answer, if only to ease the tension she was feeling. There was a whispered discussion among the three of them while Julia waited quietly, suddenly very conscious of her heart beating faster.

"Do you have pretty tits?"

The question was blunt and direct, catching her off guard but she recovered quickly.

"Most people seem to think I have."

"What do you think?"

"I think they're right."

There was a low chuckle from behind the lights.

"We'd better see if we agree, then. Remove your clothes!"

The order was so curt and brusque after the easy laughter that for a few seconds Julia felt herself hesitating then her inner resolve took over and she reached up to her blouse, fingers fumbling at the buttons.

"Slowly."

Unable to see their faces, Julia could not be sure that they weren't mocking her ready submission then she remembered that her role was to entertain them in any and every way they desired and from weeks of practice she already understood the deeply erotic message of a skilfully performed strip-tease.

Half closing her eyes against the glare of the spotlights she slowed her fingers, sliding her hands down her body between each button, stretching the fabric of the blouse against the swell of her breasts, teasing each fastening open little by little and swaying gently from side to side as she worked.

The last button came free and she worked the silk clear of the waistband of her skirt, allowing the two halves of the blouse to fall open, revealing the firm, thrusting globes of her breasts, barely contained in the fine lace nest of her bra.

No sound came from the watchers as she crossed her arms, sliding her hands back up her body, lingering briefly around her breasts, toying with the swelling buds of her nipples and then on up to her shoulders to slip the blouse free one tantalising inch at a time. Ludicrously, the thought of how the silk would crease shot briefly through her mind as she tossed it carelessly onto the stool.

Then her hands were at the fastenings of her skirt. The zipper slid easily down and that too was stripped away, rustling to the floor to be kicked to one side.

She swayed with greater abandon now, very aware of

how little cover the scraps of lace she was wearing afforded her and of how wantonly she was displaying herself. She imagined how she must look, almost naked, her firm young body shining reluctantly in the cruel glare of the lights.

Now she reached for the catch of her bra, snapping it open, feeling the weight of her breasts pulling the straps loose as she arched her back, crossing both hands in front once more and peeling the flimsy garment away. There was a faint murmur of approval, and glancing down at herself she could see her nipples swelling hard and red against her pale tan, the sight and her situation so suddenly overwhelming that she was unable to resist the impulse to caress herself, brazenly and without shame, the touch of her fingers sending small shudders rippling through her belly.

At last, and with a real effort, she dropped her hands to her thighs, half turning and raising each foot in turn onto the stool to unclip her suspenders, working the stockings slowly and carefully down her legs before reaching behind to unclip the suspender belt itself.

She was naked now, apart from the wispy lace of her panties.

She turned to face fully into the spotlight once more, hips swaying as she eased her hands, palms flat to her belly under the waistband, peeling the clinging lace down her thighs until it slipped easily to the floor and she must step free, totally naked.

"Very good. Now, kneel at the foot of the bed and listen very carefully."

As she knelt, Julia blushed at the knowledge of how she had displayed herself as she stripped and she wondered at the effect her performance had wrought on her audience. The measured tones of the speaker, a man, gave nothing away. Even though the room was warm she felt cold shivers running through her, aware that she was being drawn further and further into the control of these unknown people.

"Very soon now you will submit yourself to satisfying our demands on your body, without question or hesitation. First, you will be whipped."

As he spoke something long, black and slender was tossed in her direction and as it landed on the carpet Julia couldn't repress a shudder as she gazed down at a supple leather strap and imagined the bite of it across her naked and defenceless bottom. She had expected a thrashing, but she had also expected it to be administered by only one person. There could be no doubt that all three would want to take their turn with her, each striving to impress the others.

"H-how many strokes, please?"

She was aware that she might be committing an indiscretion but she just had to know.

"As many as we feel desirable. You will also be caned."

A whippy cane was tossed from behind the bank of lights, coming to rest beside the strap. Julia shuddered again. She could feel a familiar tingle of perverse excitement growing inside her.

"It is also necessary for you to be blindfolded and gagged."

A wide strip of black velvet sailed through the air to join the strap and the cane. She picked it up at once, tying it firmly over her eyes and blotting out the glare of the lights. All that remained now was a declaration that they intended to physically restrain her in some way and she waited quietly, forcing herself to relax.

Now that the thrashing and the inevitable gang bang which would follow was so imminent, she could feel her excitement deepening into delicious stirrings of arousal deep in her belly. Her mouth was dry and she was sure her heartbeat could be heard all around the room as she waited.

"Get to your feet and bend across the bed in a suitable position for receiving a thrashing and hold yourself in that position until we tell you otherwise."

No bondage or restraint then. In a way she would have welcomed it, knowing how difficult it could be to hold herself in a submissive posture while her bottom burned under the relentless sting of a strap. Her legs trembled so much as she got to her feet that she was sure they would not support her weight and then she turned, feeling for the bottom of the bed, spreading her legs wide and with the merest hesitation, bent right over, her forearms bent to support her upper body, her breasts hanging heavily down, erect nipples brushing lightly against the sheet.

She was as fully exposed as she could be, the lips of her sex clearly visible between her wide parted thighs and the cheeks of her bottom spread and thrust up and out behind her. Her whole body pulsed with excitement, her skin tingling in anticipation of the first touch of either hands or the strap as she heard movement behind her.

"Open your mouth."

She obeyed at once, straining her lips wide to accommodate the thick wedge of leather being pressed against them. The gag filled her mouth effective enough to stifle any sound she might make without interfering with her breathing. Someone strapped it into place. A hand strayed across her buttocks and she tensed at once, her action bringing a small chuckle of satisfaction.

"Sensitive. Very sensitive. I think we're all going to enjoy this."

"Except her!" came another voice, lighter, a woman she thought, and a finger on her buttocks made her jump.

There were more low chuckles in response and then the hand withdrew and she tensed once more, sensing that the thrashing was about to begin.

Swish!

Crack!

With incredible force the strap lashed across her offered behind, driving her forward against her braced forearms, her squeal of protest choked off by the gag, her buttocks clenching tight as she twisted and bucked in an effort to hold her pose.

Swish!

Crack!

Even as the heat of the first blow flared through her, a second whipped in, parallel to the first but lower, stinging the tender flesh where her bottom curved down into her thighs and raising her up onto her toes.

Swish, crack, again and again, hard, hard...

The strap whipped in hard and relentlessly, each new blow striping her backside with a broad, burning imprint and setting her writhing and squirming. Her hands clutched at the sheet beneath her as she fought against the urge to abandon her submissive pose and roll away from the stinging leather.

"Give me the strap."

There was a brief respite while the strap was handed over but Julia tensed as she heard the woman's voice, knowing that a woman would not be content merely to thrash away at her backside but would rather seek out her more sensitive places and whip her there. The thought sent a thrill rippling through her belly and almost without thinking she spread her legs wider and thrust her bottom higher in anticipation of what was to come and she was not disappointed.

Swish!

Crack!

Swish!

Crack!

With unerring accuracy the lash whipped in between her legs, smacking hard up against the soft and tender flesh of her inner thighs, the stinging so intense and yet so exquisite that she almost fell forward onto the bed as she bucked and twisted in an effort to hold her position.

Now the beating began to have its inevitable arousing effect on her body, the lips of her sex peeling wetly open and the musky scent of arousal pervading the air around her.

Swish!
Crack!
Swish!
Crack!

Julia squealed into her gag as the lash whipped between her thighs again and again, higher this time, the edge of the leather strap smacking right up against her sex, pain and pleasure mingling in a delicious cocktail of sensation rippling up through her belly and into her breasts, her nipples swelling quickly in response. She could feel her whole body hot and trembling, perspiration drenching her breasts as they swung wildly beneath her.

It took a real effort for her to haul herself back into her submissive posture, her bottom clenched tight and quivering in expectation of the punishment still to come.

"That's enough for now. Look how worked up she is - and we've only just started!"

Fingers probed between her thighs, feeling her wetness, and again she found herself pushing back, willing the man to penetrate her there. But already the hand was withdrawing and she moaned in frustration.

"Check her tits. Are they hard?"

She sensed movement alongside her, a slight depression of the mattress as someone sat down on the bed and then her breasts were cupped and fondled, the swollen buds of her nipples teased out between the probing fingers and she moaned again, swaying her body forward, pressing herself down onto the hands that held her. Between her thighs more fingers probed again, the lips of her sex teased out. Small shudders coursed through her as she felt her most sensitive flesh parted and stroked to the accompaniment of low murmurs of approval at her state of arousal.

Abruptly the hands fondling her so intimately withdrew and if not for the gag she would have cried out loud in an agony of frustration, her whole body tingling with arousal and aching to be penetrated.

Thwip!

Crack!

A blazing streak seared her upthrust backside and drove her down onto the bed, her legs flailing and her arms giving way beneath her as she pitched forward to lie sprawled across the sheet. She'd forgotten the cane but now as she lay panting and gasping, the thin weal reddening across the swell of her buttocks and stinging her dreadfully, she realised her tormentors intended to spare her nothing.

"Back in position! Quickly!"

Gritting her teeth Julia struggled back to her feet and resumed her submissive pose, bending as slowly as she could to avoid inflaming the welts striping her backside as her flesh was drawn taut.

"Stay like that and don't move again until we tell you."

Julia could feel her heart pounding, her legs beginning to tremble as she waited for the onslaught, not at all certain she could endure it but fearing the consequences if she did not.

Thwip!

Thwip!

Thwip!

Thwip!

The strokes whipped in without pause and with terrible force, striping Julia's pert bottom with bright red welts. Each new stroke brought a stifled howl of pain and set her bucking and heaving desperately, her knuckles white as she gripped at the sheet. This was no mere caning, this was a harsh and severe test of her fortitude and endurance, and she sobbed into her gag in a confusion of pain and fear of failure.

Her bottom felt as though it was on fire, the heat and pain of the thrashing spreading rapidly through her pliant flesh, her hips jerking and swinging wildly as if in a vain attempt to avoid the stinging cuts and still the blows rained down.

Thwip!

Thwip!

The last two strokes criss crossed her buttocks diagonally, intersecting the welts already striping her and sending even more intense shocks of pain rippling through her tortured flesh.

Then it was over and she stood, bent and trembling, her breasts swinging and heaving beneath her as she fought herself back under control. As her mind cleared from the red mist of pain she could feel the sticky wetness between her thighs, the steady throbbing in her hardened nipples and the turmoil of desire deep in her belly.

Now the straps holding her gag in place were loosened, the leather wedge pulled from her mouth as she gasped and sucked deep breaths of air into her lungs.

She longed to be taken as she stood, helpless and submissive, her bottom smarting from the savage thrashing, her body hot and glistening under the harsh glare of the spotlight.

But release was denied her.

"Bring her over here. I want her now."

There was movement beside her as Julia heard the woman's voice close by, the tones husky and urgent. Moments later she was seized, hands closing firmly under her hips and breasts as she was lifted onto the bed.

She could feel the parted thighs to either side of where she was laid, the heady musk of female arousal strong in the air around her, and she groped blindly upwards, knowing what was expected of her. The woman shifted position, sliding her belly down into Julia's questing face and sighing with satisfaction as she felt Julia's eager lips close on her sex.

Julia could taste her, feel the small contractions of pleasure rippling through her swelling lips as she sucked the pliant folds of flesh into her mouth, darting out her tongue to penetrate her, wondering if she was as naked now as she herself was, her breasts being sucked and caressed by her companions.

The woman sighed again. A long slow shudder rippled down her body and her vagina quivered between Julia's lips, the soft, wet flesh offering no resistance to her persistent, probing tongue.

"Yes, yes, lick me there, right inside, get right inside... deeper, deeper..."

Matching her actions to her urging, the woman pressed down with her feet, arching her back and thrusting her vagina more fully into Julia's perspiring face, her hips gyrating slowly and steadily in response to the stimulation she was feeling. Julia knew the other was near release and speared her tongue deep into the dripping slit, her nose and mouth full of the taste and smell of arousal. The parted lips of her own sex pulsed with desire as she drove her unseen mistress towards her climax. She could hear the low moans and gasps, feel the jerking and thrusting of the belly beneath her mouth becoming faster and more urgent and then a sudden rush of warm sticky juices seemed to flood into her mouth and it was all she could do to keep her lips clamped around the folds of quivering, pulsating flesh as the woman climaxed noisily and without abandon.

The orgasm seemed to go on and on, the belly writhing and smacking wetly against Julia's face, and then the woman fell back, still shuddering and gasping, spent and exhausted.

But for Julia there was no respite.

"Get up on your hands and knees."

She tensed as she was pulled into position, half expecting to be beaten again. Then she felt the pressure of an erect cock against her lips and understood at once, opening her mouth wide to receive it.

She could sense the man in front of her, feel the trembling of excitement in his belly as he claimed her. His thickness filled her mouth, stretching her lips wide. She felt him reaching under her to seize her hanging breasts, leaning forward into her, the better to both fondle her and hold her in place. Holding her tightly, his palms pressed flat against her nipples, he began to thrust his hips steadily back and forth, fucking her mouth as he would her vagina, each thrust reaching to the back of her throat and filling her with the taste of him.

Red faced and gasping for breath, Julia swayed before him, held captive by his grasp on her breasts, helpless to do anything other than kneel open mouthed as he took his pleasure with her, his excitement mounting rapidly and his thrusts becoming faster and faster until she felt his cock swell inside her mouth and he came, copious jets of sperm splashing back into her throat. He held her tight, his cock jammed between her lips, and she had no choice but to swallow every drop of his sperm, gagging and choking a little as the hot saltiness slipped down her throat until finally he pushed her away and she rolled over onto her side.

"On your back. Keep your legs spread."

Obediently she rolled onto her back, her legs dangling over the edge of the bed as she spread herself wide, her vagina gaping open in lewd and wanton invitation. At once she felt a hand between her thighs, the fingers probing her wetness, slipping further beneath her to explore the deep crease between her buttocks, massaging her juices into the soft flesh of her underbelly with slow insistent strokes until she could bear the exquisite sensations of her rapidly mounting desire no longer and moaned aloud, thrusting her hips clear of the bed, willing the man to penetrate her fully.

She writhed shamelessly as the man stimulated her, his fingers tracing lightly around the throbbing lips of her sex before slipping down once more into the crease of her bottom.

"Hands and knees!"

Almost sobbing with frustration, Julia rolled over and scrambled into position, her backside thrust well out and her thighs still wide parted, offering herself up to be used again, hoping that this time she would be granted the release she craved.

She heard and felt the man moving behind her, positioning himself between her thighs. He was so close that she felt his cock brush against her sex as he reached forward and under her to take a firm hold on her breasts. She pushed back against him to ease his penetration of her, but it was not her vagina he was seeking. She gasped aloud as she felt him pressing close up behind her, his cock sliding between her buttocks and coming to rest hard up against the puckered mouth of her bottom, pushing insistently at the tight opening.

She forced herself to relax, straining her thighs even wider apart, and little by little she felt herself opening up to him until with a final thrust he penetrated her fully, the whole thick length of him sliding smoothly up into her belly. For a brief moment she felt sharp pain as he impaled her and then there came a rush of pleasure as the sensitive membranes of her vagina were squeezed in on themselves and she knew her orgasm was very close.

Behind her, the man was thrusting steadily, his belly smacking against her bruised bottom with each stroke and inflaming the sharp pain of the thrashing she had received, but now the pain seemed only to spur her on to her release as she bucked and heaved beneath him.

All of her senses were concentrated on the throbbing

slit between her thighs. Then she felt her control slipping away. Long slow shudders racked her body, her heart pounding in her ears and her breath shortened to loud panting gasps.

She was dimly aware of the hands around her breasts tightening their grip and a hot wetness deep inside her as the man climaxed. Then her own orgasm claimed her, an uncontrolled rush of pleasure that seemed to go on and on until she collapsed and lay limp and exhausted on the bed.

Chapter Nine

A finger prodded Julia in the ribs and she stirred, rolling over onto her side and curling up.

The finger prodded again, harder this time and Julia yelped, rolling away out of reach and yelping again as her bruised and sore buttocks bounced off the sheet.

"Up!"

It was the woman!

With the blindfold still secured tightly in place, Julia cast around in the direction of the voice, recognising it as that of the woman in the trio she had so recently satisfied. Obviously they had not been satisfied enough, merely waiting until she had recovered before starting in on her again. Her muscles tightened as she lay still, waiting for the next order.

"You can remove the blindfold if you wish."

Eagerly she reached up. Her fingers fumbled at the knot behind her head until it fell away and she lay blinking in the sudden rush of light. The room was still lit only by the bank of spotlights trained on the bed, illuminating her while effectively rendering anyone sitting on the other side a vague blur.

"Sit up and let me look at you properly."

Julia pushed herself into a sitting position, squinting into the light as she did so. She could discern only one figure and glanced around quickly for the other two.

"We are alone now. Just you and me."

That fact did not reassure Julia. Of the three of them it had been the woman who had beaten her the most effectively and cruelly. She wondered if the woman was still naked and glanced down at her own body, already so thoroughly ravaged from her earlier activities. She had to admit it was not a very modest or demure sight. Her breasts and nipples were still reddened from the constant fondling and her belly and thighs were slicked with thin trails of sperm in clear evidence of how the men had used her. Her mouth still carried the sharp, salty tang of sperm where she had sucked one of them off and an errant dribble clung to her lips.

She sat very still although her heart was beginning to beat faster and faster with each minute that passed.

"Get yourself cleaned up."

Julia staggered to her feet and headed for the small en suite bathroom.

"Leave the door open."

Julia didn't care who watched her, she was already fiddling with the mixer tap on the shower to send a warm, soothing spray cascading over her body. There was soap and scented oils in plentiful supply and she used them all, emerging from the bathroom ten minutes later thoroughly clean, her skin glowing and tingling where she had towelled herself vigorously dry.

In her brief absence the spotlights had been switched off and replaced by the altogether softer glow of the standard room lights, allowing her to see clearly the woman waiting for her. She was younger than Julia had expected, perhaps only in her mid thirties, but radiating an aura of success and power. She was a picture of elegance, her short auburn hair brushed to a glossy sheen, her make up immaculate, softening the otherwise sharp and severe lines of her face. Her silk robe was loosely belted to give a tantalising glimpse of the firm curves of her body beneath, her long bare legs elegantly crossed as she waited. Julia envied her cool, relaxed poise, suddenly very aware of her own utter nakedness as the woman submitted her to a searching scrutiny.

"Stand over there and clasp your hands behind your head."

Julia moved to the middle of the room and took up the required pose, the action at once lifting and tightening her breasts.

"Turn. Slowly."

Again Julia obeyed, her cheeks beginning to flush hot under the woman's searching gaze until she had turned in a full circle and stood facing her once more.

"You seem fairly fit. Do you exercise?"

"Yes, almost every day."

The woman regarded her silently for a few more minutes, her eyes lingering on every inch of Julia's nude body then she rose from her chair.

"Come and stand in front of me."

Her voice was calm yet commanding, and Julia felt a surge of helplessness as she obeyed. Apart from Natalie, who was backed by the power of Nico's organisation, Julia had never experienced such authority and self confidence in another woman. There was no doubt that this woman was accustomed to instant obedience and no question at all in her mind that Julia would submit herself utterly to her wishes.

"Do you know who I am, Julia?"

"No."

"Don't you read the papers?"

The woman's voice was sharper, edged with wounded pride and Julia feared she had committed an indiscretion.

"No. I don't seem to have the time."

It sounded such a feeble excuse but it sufficed.

"I suppose maybe you don't. Well for the record, my name is Marsha Masterman, that's Miss Masterman to you, and I've just been appointed head prosecutor for the state."

"I see."

She sounded proud of the appointment and Julia did her best to sound impressed.

"What was that?"

Her voice was sharp again, demanding, and Julia felt suddenly flustered.

"I-I mean, I see, Miss Masterman."

"That's better."

Marsha relaxed again and Julia breathed a silent sigh of relief. She was going to have to be very careful. Obviously this woman was quick to take offence and she wasn't in any position to take unnecessary risks.

"Perhaps Mistress would be a more suitable form of address?"

Julia waited dry mouthed as Marsha pondered the question, a wicked smile playing at the corners of her mouth.

"Yes, definitely, I think I prefer Mistress... how about you?"

"Yes Miss... er... Mistress. Yes, that's definitely better."

Julia was learning fast, although she despised herself for her ready and craven agreement to whatever this woman asked of her. She barely flinched as Marsha reached out and took hold of her breast although her nipples began to swell almost at once.

"Sensitive, aren't you?"

"Yes, Mistress."

Marsha was caressing the captive breasts, squeezing gently at the firm, rounded globes, her eyes sparkling as she watched the erotic effect her touch was provoking.

"Such attractive nipples too, I bet men just can't resist playing with them."

Marsha was toying with them herself, pulling the hot, swelling buds out from her body and twisting them hard until Julia gasped out loud. She felt her legs beginning to tremble, a warm liquid feeling stirring in her belly as her nipples swelled ever larger and harder under the persistent stimulation. She could feel the heat rising inside her and wondered if Marsha could sense it. Her breath quickened, her breasts beginning to heave and her legs trembling almost uncontrollably.

"Yes, really very sensitive. Turn around."

Julia turned around, thankful that the teasing stimulation of her breasts had stopped before she disgraced herself.

"Now bend forward and touch your toes."

Julia knew that once bent over in such a submissive posture there could be no way of hiding her aroused condition, but had no choice other than to obey at once. Gritting her teeth against the lewd exposure, Julia bent slowly forward until she could grasp her ankles, presenting Marsha with a clear view of both her sex and her so cruelly punished backside.

Smack!

The sharp slap drew a yelp of pain from her lips and her buttocks quivered from the sudden impact.

"I said touch your toes, not your ankles!"

"S-sorry, Mistress."

Julia resumed her position and forced herself further forward until her outstretched fingers brushed firmly against her toes. Getting down to the position was not too great a problem, but holding it certainly was. Already she could feel the strain in her legs and she shuffled her feet further apart in search of relief.

Her backside was a taut quivering curve jutting out behind her, the stripes where she had been beaten vivid against the pale tan of her skin. Marsha trailed her fingers lightly along those stripes, smiling to herself as Julia struggled to control her reactions. She was fighting a losing battle with her body. Her submissive posture and shameless exposure, and the persistent stimulation of Marsha's busy fingers, all combined to send tremors of arousal rippling through her belly. Between her legs she could feel herself warm and wet, the lips of her sex peeling ever so slowly apart to betray her mounting excitement.

"Getting worked up, are we?"

Marsha slid her fingers between Julia's parted thighs, feeling the soft wet folds of flesh throbbing and swelling at her touch. Julia moaned softly, swaying back against the intruding fingers, willing Marsha to penetrate her and shame her in a glorious flood of orgasm.

"Up!"

Julia moaned again, her frustration very evident in the quivering of her sex and the hardness of her nipples. Her whole body was hot and alive with arousal but the relief she craved was denied.

"Turn around. Look at me."

Julia turned, her breasts heaving as she fought herself back under control. Marsha was naked, the silk robe thrown carelessly over the chair, her own nipples very hard and erect, straining out from breasts that were full and rounded. In contrast, the rest of her body was lean and well toned, her belly flat and firm and her legs long and slender. Julia thought she looked like an amazon, proud and dominant, her looks matching her mood.

"You'll come when and if I decide!"

"Yes, Mistress."

Marsha smiled, a wicked smile that sent a cold spasm deep into Julia's belly.

"Now, make me come - and make it good."

Striding past Julia she flung herself full length onto the bed, rolling onto her back, legs parted and outstretched.

Julia hesitated for only a moment before climbing onto the bed, kneeling between Marsha's parted legs, her tongue running quickly around her lips. Marsha watched her through half closed eyes, her hands already stroking over the firm curves of her breasts.

"Lick me slowly. Make it last."

Julia looked down at her lying back so open and wanton and demanding, the thick bush of dark auburn hair at the apex of her parted thighs barely concealing the waiting lips of her sex. She licked her lips again and bent forward, running her tongue lightly up the length of Marsha's inner thigh, feeling the warm flesh rippling under her caress.

"Mmmmmm... again!"

Marsha wriggled her hips, settling herself closer to Julia's questing lips and tongue, her fingers busy at her breasts. Her skin was soft and scented, quivering gently under the touch of Julia's lips and tongue. She parted her legs wider, thrusting her hips forward, her sex already open and moist.

Julia trailed her lips obediently up the inside of one smooth skinned thigh, lingered a little just below the quivering slit of Marsha's sex, and then darted forward, flicking her tongue wetly around the waiting lips.

Marsha shuddered at once, lifting her hips clear of the bed and thrusting her belly towards Julia's mouth. The heady musk of her arousal hung heavily in the air, warm dampness spreading quickly between her parted thighs.

"Again. Again."

Marsha's voice was husky and breathless, her excitement mounting rapidly as Julia tongued the now dripping lips of her sex.

"Get your tongue inside me... right inside..."

Marsha's hips began to gyrate in long, slow circles as Julia pressed her lips around the gaping mouth of her sex and thrust her tongue deep into the hot wet pit of her belly. Marsha's reaction was immediate, almost tossing Julia aside as she writhed and squirmed, her breath shallow and rasping, hips bouncing on the bed.

Julia hung on, clamping her lips firmly around Marsha's

sex and sucking the distended lips deep into her mouth. Her tongue speared deeper, hungrily lapping up the freely flowing juices and Marsha went wild above her. Her hips bucked and heaved madly, her belly smacking wetly against Julia's face and her breasts bouncing.

"Yes, yes, deeper, deeper..."

The woman's excitement was mounting even higher, her control slipping rapidly away. Her body was hot and vibrant, her orgasm suddenly flooding through her, the uncontrollable sensations gripping her body somehow transmitting themselves to Julia as her heaving became even more frenzied. Julia hung on, lashing at the hot pulsating flesh with her tongue, sucking the swollen and dripping lips back into her mouth, her own body shuddering in time to Marsha's frenzied gyrations. The sharp tang of arousal filled her mouth as she lapped up the now freely flowing juices, the sticky excess dribbling out from between her lips and trickling down her chin.

Beneath her she could feel her breasts bouncing on the bed, nipples tingling as they rubbed across the silky sheets and she pressed forward eagerly, tongue darting deep inside Marsha's still throbbing slit.

It was as though they had become one, Marsha squirming and twisting on her back as she climaxed again and again while Julia lay writhing between her thighs. She longed to reach down, to burrow her hands beneath her belly and plunge her fingers into her own wet and throbbing slit. Her own breathing was becoming laboured, her face flushed red and glistening with perspiration and she could feel herself becoming more and more aroused as she writhed on the sheet.

Above her, Marsha was still racked by the spasms of her orgasm. Julia wondered if she would even notice if she herself gave in to the passions building inside her. She squeezed her thighs together, gasping at the sharp spasm that rippled up through her belly in instant response. Another squeeze, harder and held for longer and she gasped again, the sweet feeling of release welling up inside her.

"Enough! Enough!"

Marsha thrust her hands down, pushing Julia away, her body still shuddering and trembling in the aftermath of the orgasms that had racked her. Julia was trembling too, her body alive with arousal and frustration as she lay face down between Marsha's thighs. The temptation to thrust her fingers into her belly and bring herself to a shattering climax was almost irresistible but she fought against it as she had been ordered to do.

For a long time the only sound in the room was Marsha's laboured breathing. Gradually Julia's feelings of frustration ebbed away and were replaced by the glow of relief that she had evidently satisfied the other's demands.

"Up."

Julia pushed herself shakily to her knees as Marsha laid back and watched, a lazy smile on her lips.

"Natalie said you were good, she just didn't say how good."

"Thank you, Mistress."

It seemed ridiculous to thank the woman for doing something she herself had wanted but Julia understood that a little show of humility could often go a long way.

"That's all right, Julia, I'm sure we'll get along just fine together."

"Yes, Mistress."

Without another word, Marsha slid from the bed and headed for the bathroom, closing the door firmly behind her. Julia could hear the sound of running water, but remained kneeling where she was. She had not been told to move. It was the right decision for when Marsha stepped back into the room a few minutes later she nodded approval.

"Obedient too, it seems."

Julia continued to wait, hearing the woman dressing behind her but not willing to turn around to watch.

"You can get up now, Julia, and turn around."

Julia turned to be confronted by Marsha, fully dressed in an obviously expensive designer outfit. She looked every inch the successful career woman, confident and composed as though she had just finished a business meeting.

"I think you could benefit from a little extra exercise, Julia, and I'll be in touch with you soon."

"Yes, Mistress."

"Apart from that we're finished for the evening although the room is reserved and paid for until tomorrow morning if you wish to stay here. You certainly look as though you need the rest."

She smiled thinly at her own joke and left without another word, the door closing quietly behind her.

Chapter Ten

If Julia expected to be given some time to recover from the rigours of her introduction to Marsha and her friends, she soon discovered otherwise, for the woman called her just after lunch the following day.

"Ah, Julia, about that exercise program we discussed last night."

It hadn't exactly been a discussion but there was no stopping Marsha.

"I've arranged a private session at a gym for this afternoon. I'll meet you there in about an hour."

She gave the address and rang off at once leaving Julia staring dumbly at the telephone. As if she hadn't already guessed, Marsha had all the makings of a hard task mistress and she hurried through her preparations. The driver of the cab she hailed knew the address but he glanced quizzically at her as she gave it.

"You sure you want to go there, lady."

"Yes, why not?"

He shrugged. "It's a rough neighbourhood, not the sort of place I'd usually take a smart young girl like you."

He shrugged again and pulled out into the traffic as Julia sat back. The driver was right. It certainly wasn't the sort of area she would willingly frequent. The smart modern buildings of the city centre gave way to ever more shabby and neglected neighbourhoods, until at last the cab drew up in front of the gym. It was in sharp contrast to the stylish aerobic studio she was accustomed to using, situated on the corner of what seemed like a particularly seedy and neglected street of commercial property. A group of men were lounging near the corner, drinking from bottles. Sacks of rubbish spilled untidily onto the sidewalk around them.

"Are you really sure, lady?"

Julia checked the address in the hope the driver had made a mistake before climbing nervously from the cab, hurrying into the dingy doorway as quickly as she could. The gym was as dingy and run down inside as it appeared from the outside, and Julia was certain that she must have made a mistake in copying the address. She was on the point of leaving when she heard the now familiar voice of Marsha.

"You're late!"

Julia felt flustered and a little upset at the unfairness of the accusation, especially as it was less than an hour since Marsha had called her.

"I'm sorry, I got here as quickly as I could."

"Forget the excuses, girl, just get yourself in here."

Julia stepped into the gym and looked around her. Marsha was lounging against a piece of apparatus. She was dressed in a safari jacket and a short skirt that displayed her slim legs to perfection, and Julia felt suddenly dowdy alongside Marsha's elegant designer outfit. There was an attendant too, young and good looking and also wearing sweat shirt and shorts.

"Changing rooms are over there."

He locked the door to the street behind her and jerked a thumb in the direction of a short corridor leading off from the gym.

"I'll come with you."

Marsha strode across the room and Julia shrugged resignedly as she followed along behind. The changing room was in keeping with the rest of the building, grubby and smelling of stale sweat, and Marsha wrinkled her nose in distaste.

"It's certainly no palace but I'm afraid it's the best I could arrange at short notice and at least we won't be disturbed."

Julia became even more nervous as the woman settled down to watch her change.

"You have quite a good figure, Julia. Don't you think so?"

"I... well, I suppose so, Miss."

Julia stripped quickly and was reaching for her leotard when Marsha stopped her.

"No need to bother with that there's only me to see you. And Ricky, of course but I'm sure that doesn't give you any problem."

Julia felt her stomach sinking and opened her mouth to protest before realising that any objections she had would be brushed aside. Worse than that was the likelihood of annoying Marsha, who was now smiling openly at her discomfort.

"It doesn't worry you, does it?"

"N-no-"

Julia despised herself for her ready submission and she cast a longing look at the leotard lying on the bench as Marsha got to her feet and led her back to the gym. Ricky's eyes lit up as he saw Julia, his gaze lingering appreciatively on the proud swell of her breasts and her smooth shaven mound. His eyes widened even more when he caught sight of the welts striping her buttocks and thighs. Julia was fit and the marks were fading quickly, but it was still very obvious that she had been beaten recently.

Marsha waited, content to prolong Julia's humiliation as Ricky walked slowly round her, inspecting her closely from every angle until at last he stood facing her once more.

"A full work out, Miss Masterman?"

"Absolutely. Julia looks quite fit, but she's actually out of condition, so make sure it's good and hard."

Marsha was grinning openly and Julia could see from the very obvious bulge in the front of Ricky's shorts that the work out was not the only thing good and hard. From past experience she guessed that sooner or later she was going to have to do something about that, but for now she waited for instructions, eyeing the equipment scattered about the room with a growing sense of unease.

"Before we start, hold out your arms."

Julia felt even more uneasy as Marsha dug into the pocket of her jacket and produced two pairs of handcuffs. Deftly, she snapped a pair around each of Julia's proffered wrists and stepped back, nodding to Ricky.

"Right. She's all yours."

The warm up routines that Ricky put her through were easy and familiar, but Julia felt acutely embarrassed at carrying them out naked and under his lecherous gaze. She had to part her legs then stretch and bend to touch her toes, very aware of the young man positioning himself to catch a clear view of her breasts as they swung freely. From where he was standing as he called out the tempo of the exercise, he also had an uninterrupted view of her sex each time she bent over.

With her legs parted, she was unable to prevent the lips opening and she blushed furiously at the exhibition she knew she was giving. Ricky sensed her embarrassment and made it worse by ordering her to hold the pose for several seconds before straightening up each time.

Marsha lounged against the wall, watching with an almost bored expression until Ricky signalled that the warm up was over and that it was time for the real exercises to begin. He beckoned Julia towards a jogging machine, motioning her to stand up on the conveyor belt and reaching out for her arms.

Julia now realised why Marsha had cuffed her wrists, for it was the work of a few moments for him to snap the dangling half of each cuff around the rails on either side of the belt. However arduous and for however long the exercise, she now had no choice but to finish it and, to complete her sense of anxiety, she was also helpless to prevent Ricky touching her up.

Already excited at the sight of her stretching and bending so shamelessly in the warm up, he took full advantage, running his hands eagerly across her breasts and down the flat plane of her stomach, fingers probing between her thighs. At first she murmured in protest but her body betrayed her. Her nipples hardened and swelled at his touch and warmth and dampness spread between her legs as he teased her until her murmurs gave way to low moans and she began to writhe up against him.

"I think that's enough for now, Ricky. She's starting to enjoy herself too much."

"You're right, Miss Masterman!"

He held up his hand, fingers wet with Julia's juices, and a broad smile spread across his face.

"Maybe later you and me can have a little fun, my girl, but for now I'm afraid you're going to have to work out like the lady says."

He reached for the switch and set the belt in motion and Julia took up the pace, her gaze fixed determinedly ahead to avoid displaying her frustrated expression. The pace was easy, no more than a brisk walk, but after a few moments she was dismayed to see Ricky reaching for the switch and clicking it round onto a faster setting. Twice more he adjusted the speed until the pace was set at a brisk jog and Julia began to feel the effort.

With each stride her bare breasts bounced and jiggled and her breathing quickened in response to the pace. Perspiration began to glisten on her body and her breathing shortened to quick, panting gasps. Both Ricky and Marsha were watching her closely and she kept her gaze fixed ahead, concentrating on maintaining a steady rhythm.

"Faster!"

Julia gasped with dismay but was powerless to prevent Ricky clicking the switch round one more notch. She was running now, legs stretching and feet pounding on the belt. Her breasts bounced and swung uncomfortably from side to side with each step and her breath rasped harshly in her throat. Perspiration bathed her whole body, trickling down her face and half blinding her, and her feet began to slip on the fast moving belt.

Twice she stumbled and would have fallen headlong but for the cuffs shackling her to the machine. The pace did not ease. She could feel her heart pounding, the muscles in her legs aching with each stride. Ricky and Marsha had ceased to exist. Nothing existed but the endlessly moving belt and the pounding of her heart. Twice more she faltered, convinced she was about to pass out from the effort...

And then, almost unbelievably, the belt began to slow.

One notch at a time, Ricky clicked the switch back round to the stop. Breasts heaving, she gasped for breath, her whole body hot and dripping with sweat and her legs hardly able to hold her up.

"Looks like she could do with a rest."

Julia turned to look at Marsha, blinking the mist of perspiration from her eyes, hardly daring to believe that the session might be over.

"I've got just the set up over here, Miss Masterman."

Ricky was still grinning as he unlocked the cuffs from the machine and led her on still trembling legs, towards a low, padded bench.

"Here's where you get to lie down for a while."

She was in no condition to resist as Ricky pushed her firmly down onto her back on the narrow bench. Her legs were parted and dangled on either side and she blushed furiously at the thought of how exposed she was. Ricky rummaged around in a rack under the bench and produced two stubby dumbbells.

"Let me have your arms."

Pulling her arms out to the side, he made sure she grasped each dumbbell securely before snapping the cuffs around the handles. The weights were heavy and dragged down towards the floor, her breasts straining up from her chest as she struggled to keep her arms outstretched. Ricky grasped her wrists bringing her arms up above her supine body, banging the weights together then lowering her arms almost to the floor again.

"That's all you have to do, Julia and it's a great exercise for improving your tits."

He chuckled and stepped back as Julia sucked in her breath, struggling to raise the weights as he had done.

"Try for twenty?"

Marsha nodded agreement and Julia almost sobbed out loud. Already her arms were aching just with the effort of holding the weights and twenty lifts seemed way beyond reach.

"Come on, Julia. The longer you take the harder it gets."

Sucking in another deep breath, Julia swung her arms upwards, her gaze fixed on the ceiling, concentrating hard. The movement was ragged, but the dumbbells banged together and she let her arms fall back, gathering herself for the next lift. After five lifts it began to get harder, the weights dragging at her arms and by fifteen she was struggling even to raise her arms high enough. Her muscles ached with an intensity she had never felt before and she longed for a break.

Ricky straddled the bench, his expression mocking as he looked down at her. Her arms were dragged right back, the dumbbells resting on the floor as she struggled to raise them and her breasts strained up towards him. Despite her fatigue, her nipples were hard and erect, and he couldn't resist reaching down, fingertips flicking across them.

"Come on now. No slacking."

His fingers flicked at her again, harder, the sharp contact drawing quick gasps from her as she hauled her arms straight.

"I can't... too heavy..."

"Make the twenty or you go back on the treadmill before you try again."

Julia shuddered and strained harder, finally succeeding in bringing the weights together again.

"Only four more."

Only! Gritting her teeth, Julia hauled her arms up. She was quivering all over with the effort, every muscle screaming. Ricky reached for her breasts once more, squeezing the firm mounds in both hands as she struggled to complete the task. Her nipples rubbed insistently against his palms and she could feel herself becoming aroused, her concentration slipping away. Desperately she sucked in her breath and made a supreme effort. The weights touched above her head, once, twice, three and finally, arms trembling, four times.

Limply she sagged back, uncaring of the drag on her arms and shoulders or of Ricky enthusiastically massaging her straining hard nippled breasts. She was sure she could take no more. All that was left was for Ricky to fuck her as she lay on the bench and she knew she did not have the will or the strength to resist. Marsha looked down at her, a smile of satisfaction on her lips.

"Exhausted?"

"Yes."

It was all Julia could do to whisper the reply, her breasts still heaving as she gasped for breath.

"Perhaps one more routine?"

"Oh, no... please... I can't."

Julia moaned in despair, hardly able to stir from the bench, let alone carry out more arduous exercise, and Marsha shook her head.

"You disappoint me, Julia. I thought you were much fitter than that."

Julia moaned weakly, eyes closed so she did not see Marsha reaching into her pocket once more. She pulled out a short leather strap and positioned herself at the foot of the bench between Julia's limply dangling thighs. Ricky's eyes widened and he too moved closer, licking his lips in anticipation of what he was about to witness.

Swish!

Crack!

With savage precision, Marsha lashed the strap down on Julia's prostrate body, striking at the tender flesh of her inner thigh, close up against the parted lips of her sex. Julia yelped, eyes snapping open, hips jerking up against the unexpected jolt of pain.

Swish!

Crack!

Marsha struck again and again Julia yelped and squirmed. With her legs dangling to either side of the bench and the heavy dumbbells still shackled to her wrists she was helpless to avoid the stinging blows.

Swish!

Crack!

Swish!

Crack!

Marsha switched her aim, smacking the strap sharply down along Julia's belly, two narrow welts reddening darkly across the swell of her pubic mound. Julia howled, writhing desperately in a vain attempt to avoid the stinging blows, tears springing from her eyes at the cruel torment.

Swish!

Crack!

Swish!

Crack!

Marsha laid the lash hard up against Julia's open sex and Julia howled louder, her hips bouncing against the bench as the savage pain bit into her most sensitive flesh. Marsha and Ricky looked on with wide eyed fascination as she bucked and heaved, the lips of her sex darkening to a deep, angry red where the lash had struck, but also swelling and glistening with the first flush of arousal. Marsha stepped back, replaced the strap in her pocket and waited until Julia's writhing had subsided.

"I knew you weren't as exhausted as you looked."

Julia gazed up at her pleadingly. Her sex and belly stung dreadfully and she could see Ricky watching her lustfully. She could hardly blame him. Her nipples stood out hard and swollen from her heaving breasts and between her thighs she could feel herself open and wet. Her hips and belly still quivered in the aftermath of the beating, the welts striping her and drawing attention to her sex.

"I'll leave you with Ricky now and he'll work out an exercise program for you."

Julia nodded weakly, knowing that the moment Marsha left the gym, Ricky would waste no time in fucking her. At least that would be the end of the punishing fitness routine.

"As for you, Julia, I'm sure we'll meet again before very long and we'll have some real fun together."

She turned to leave, and Ricky followed her to unlock the door, and Julia felt a familiar tingle of excitement rushing through her as he locked the door again and walked slowly back towards her. His erection was very obvious, straining against the thin fabric of his shorts. Standing at the end of the bench, he pulled them down, his cock springing free, thick and throbbing. Julia peered down between her breasts, watching him, her heart beginning to beat faster.

"Marsha says you're a real good fuck, Julia, is that

right?"

Julia said nothing and he shrugged casually.

"Well, I guess I'm going to find out for myself."

He sat straddling the bench, his knees pushing her legs wider apart. The vivid welts where Marsha had whipped her fascinated him and he trailed his fingers up the inside of her thighs and across her belly, tracing along the still stinging tracks. Julia winced at his touch and then his fingers dived down between her thighs, circling the wet and inviting lips of her sex and she gasped out loud.

"You want it, don't you. You want me to fuck you?

"Yes! Yes!"

Her ready admission shamed her but she couldn't help herself squirming against his probing fingers as he delved deeper and deeper inside her belly. Almost casually he reached under her spread thighs, lifting her bottom clear of the bench and leaning forward, the better to penetrate her. His throbbing cock hovered above her belly and she felt the excitement rising inside her as she peered down at him between the straining swell of her breasts.

He pulled her legs wider, pushing his own thighs under hers to hold her up, lifting her higher. His cock brushed up against the pulsing lips of her sex and in one smooth movement he bent forward and entered her, hands reaching out to grasp her breasts as he slid easily into her.

Julia shuddered, the thick, hardness of him stretching her wide and her nipples tingling as his fingers closed around them. His belly pressed down hard on hers, inflaming the two welts striping her there but the sharp pain proved an added spur to her arousal as she squirmed against him. She knew he was excited, could feel the first urgent pulsations in his cock as he thrust strongly into her.

The fear that he would climax too soon gripped her and she thrust herself towards him, dragging him deeper into the hot, yearning pit of her sex. Her nipples throbbed as he fondled them, short spasms of pleasure darting through her breasts, and she felt her control slipping away. Arching her back she pressed herself against the cock thrusting inside her, feeling the dripping walls of her sex contracting around the thick shaft as the first wave of orgasm surged through her.

It no longer mattered who was fucking her, all that mattered was the surge of release flooding her belly as she climaxed, writhing and gasping with total abandon. Ricky gasped too, his body suddenly stiffening against her, hands gripping her breasts hard as spasms of release racked him. His sperm jetted out, filling her sex as his cock jerked uncontrollably inside her. Still gasping he collapsed forward on top of her pressing her down onto the bench as the last spasms of orgasm rippled through her and she lay, hot and panting, totally spent beneath him.

Chapter Eleven

Almost half an hour passed as Julia lay exposed on the bench, but all the while she knew that Ricky was watching her closely. Several times he reached out to stroke her breasts or slide his fingers along the soft flesh of her inner thighs, but she was so exhausted that his touch failed to rouse her to anything more than a low moan. He shrugged and rose from the bench, bending down to unlock the cuffs still fastening the heavy dumbbells to her wrists. She stirred then, bringing her aching arms up by her side onto the bench, a soft sigh of relief escaping from her lips.

"So, you're awake after all?"

She opened her eyes and looked at him, her expression wary.

"Can I get up now?"

"Sure, you're all finished for today and I need to open up the gym soon."

She hauled herself upright, wincing at the aches that seemed to pervade her whole body and Ricky grinned again.

"A few days of the exercise program I'm going to give you and you'll feel really great."

She glanced up at him, her expression now tired and resigned.

"Do I have to come here to work out?"

"Well, Marsha didn't say, so I guess not."

Julia nodded, noting the look of disappointment on the young man's face. She was relieved that she would be able to work through the exercise routines in her regular gym and at her own pace, but at the same time she too felt a strange sense of disappointment. It was true that he had fucked her only because she was naked and available, but it had been a long time since she had been fucked by such a young man.

He was hardly more than a boy, she realised as she looked at him more closely. After months of being made to satisfy men, many years older than herself, almost all of them unfit, some of them fat and balding, there was something appealing about the thought of sex with someone nearer her own age.

As she struggled with her thoughts he turned away and she felt a sudden urge to call him back and offer herself shamelessly to be used by him. But the words wouldn't come and she sank back on the bench feeling foolish.

"You'd better clean yourself up and get dressed. I have to open up the gym in just under an hour."

She sighed as he left the gym and levered herself to her feet, wincing once more as the aching aftermath of the hectic afternoon gripped her. On shaking legs she made her way back to the changing room and staggered into the open shower stall. The water was icy cold and she jumped back as it hit her, shivering and gasping for breath, fumbling for the mixer tap.

Inevitably, given the run down state of the rest of the building, the tap was broken. The shower dispensed an icy spray whatever setting she chose. She gritted her teeth and stepped under it, gasping out loud as the water cascaded down her body. There was no soap, but she rubbed herself all over, washing the sweat and sperm from her body. The cold spray revived her physically. Her whole body tingled and glowed and as she turned under the spray, she saw Ricky watching her from the doorway. She wondered how long he had been silently watching her, but she felt no shame as she faced him, making no attempt to hide her nakedness.

"I brought your work-out routine."

He dropped a sheet of paper onto the bench beside her clothes, but his eyes never left her body. She imagined how she must appear to him, her body wet and glistening, nipples shrivelled into tight hard buds and the thin red marks where Marsha had whipped her showing vivid on her belly and thighs. A tell tale bulge strained at the front of his shorts and she felt suddenly breathless at the thought that they were still alone together in the gym with almost an hour before anyone else was likely to arrive. He had fucked her once and there was nothing to prevent him doing so again.

She was sure that was what he wanted, for he made no effort to conceal his bulging erection. His eyes roamed avidly over her nakedness. With a shock that jolted her, she suddenly realised that she wanted him too, wanted him thrusting hard into her sex, his mouth on her breasts, his strong hands gripping her, holding her down while he fucked her to an explosive climax.

The thought was so intense that for a few moments she stood rooted to the spot. Her heart pounded and she realised that here, in this grubby gym, for the first time in months, she was actually choosing to submit to the desires of a man who wanted her because she herself wanted him.

She licked her lips as a tingle of wicked anticipation stirred in her belly, and stepped quickly from the shower, water dripping heedlessly from her body. Her clothes and her bag were right next to where he was standing. All she had to do was walk across the room and she knew he would be unable to resist the temptation to grab her.

Her mouth felt suddenly dry and her legs shook. Neither Nico nor Natalie would approve of what she was doing, but that just added to the excitement now coursing through her. She was going to be fucked, she was sure of it, and she was really relishing the prospect.

She reached her bag, turning slightly as she bent to open it, allowing Ricky a good view of her breasts as they swung gently with her movement. The tension was almost unbearable and she wondered if she should turn to him, offering herself...

And then he grabbed for her.

His hands closed around her waist, gripping tight, spinning her round to face him. Her wet feet skidded on the floor so that she stumbled, almost fell, and then his hand closed around her breast, squeezing hard, steadying her against him. At once her nipples began to harden and swell and she pressed herself blatantly closer to him, making no secret of her response to his touch.

He looked down at her and she watched his eyes widen with sudden understanding as he saw the wanton desire written on her face.

"Do it to me..."

Her voice sounded husky and breathless as she writhed against him, grinding her breast into his clutching palm, feeling the nipple tingling as her desire for him grew.

His eyes shone with excitement as he released her breast, shoving both hands under the waistband of his shorts. His cock sprang free, thrusting up towards her, already hard and stiff. She reached down for him, encircling him in her eager fingers, then glanced up at him, her smile both wicked and excited.

Now she dropped to her knees.

She ran her tongue quickly around her lips, opening her mouth wide, holding him firmly as she leaned in towards him.

A shudder of excitement raced through his body as he realised what she was doing. He leaned forward into her, bracing his hands against the wall. As she sucked him eagerly into her mouth, Julia could feel his excitement in the steady pulsing of the rod of flesh. The smell and taste of his arousal made her heart beat faster. Between her legs she could feel herself becoming hot and wet, the soft folds of flesh shielding her vagina peeling irresistibly open.

She drew back her head, allowing him almost to slip free of her lips, teasing him with her tongue before plunging forward again. His cock speared to the back of her throat and her breasts swung heavily against his legs.

Her nipples swelled still harder, short spasms of pleasure tingled in her breasts as she held him deep in her mouth, sucking hard, rubbing herself up against him. She knew he was watching her from between his braced arms. She could feel his arousal growing with each moment she held him in her mouth. Her hands dropped to her belly, probing between her thighs, fingers gripping the swelling, fleshy lips, opening herself wider. She knew he could see her. She felt the sharp spasm of excitement rippling through his cock as she touched herself.

She had wanted him to penetrate her, but now she knew that she could make him come in her mouth while she masturbated. The thought sent a shiver of excitement rippling through her belly. She drew back her head and prepared to plunge back down onto his throbbing shaft for the final time, her fingers delving into her sex, driving herself towards an orgasm that she knew would flood through her the instant he climaxed into her throat.

"No, no, not yet..."

Ricky stepped back, his cock springing loose from her lips and swaying wetly in front of her face. Desperately she lunged forward, seeking to capture him again, gasping with need and desire.

"Up! Up! Get up!"

Ricky grabbed her arms, hauling her to her feet, his red and sweat streaked face just inches from her own. She hung limply in his grip, breasts heaving as she gasped for breath.

"You randy bitch!"

He slammed her back against the wall, his eyes wild and his chest heaving, his mouth coming down to close on hers as his hands dropped to her hips. His tongue forced her lips apart and she responded eagerly, thrusting her hips towards him. His hands slid over her buttocks, gripping hard, pulling her legs apart. His cock pressed against her belly, still hot and throbbing and then she felt him lifting her, his cock sliding down towards her slit. Her movements were instinctive, her arms going around his neck, supporting herself as he lifted her higher. His cock slipped between her thighs, slid into the furrow of her sex and she squealed softly, pressing herself against his chest.

For a long drawn out moment he held her poised, cock swaying at the yearning mouth of her belly then he relaxed his grip and thrust up hard, impaling her as she dropped. She squealed again, squirming hard against his chest as a spasm of pleasure gripped her. He was filling her completely, his thickness forcing her wide. She could feel the distended bud of her clitoris bearing down on the flaring base of his shaft, each movement no matter how small translating into shocks of pleasure.

He was pulling at her bottom now, opening her thighs wider, driving himself deeper. Her feet were clear of the floor and she dangled impaled, his weight crushing her breasts into her ribs as he pressed her back against the wall. Her nipples were circles of pure sensation and she could feel him penetrating deeper and deeper into her. She couldn't hold out any longer. She could feel the cock swelling inside her, long slow contractions rippling along it's length but her own dam broke first. The sharp, hot spasms from her belly met the spasms radiating out from her breasts and she climaxed, shuddering and moaning, her juices bathing the cock thrust so deep inside her and spilling out onto her thighs. She knew Ricky was coming too, felt the sudden swelling and spasmodic jerking of his cock as he spurted his semen up into her, gathering up the tail end of her first orgasm and driving her to another shattering climax.

Her hips bucked and jerked against his, her cries of passion muffled by his lips pressed on hers, her breasts bounced and heaved against his broad chest as she spent herself in an orgy of wanton abandon.

Ricky held her tight, emptying himself into her, revelling in the feel of her writhing against him with such wildness. His cock was shrinking rapidly and as he finally slipped free of her she gave a last convulsive shudder and fell limply against him...

"Time to go."

Julia whimpered softly, still quivering in the afterglow of her orgasms and made no show of resistance as Ricky led her back to the shower. They showered together, Ricky washing the sweat and semen from her body while she stood passive and docile and afterwards he watched her as she dressed.

"If you want to work out here any time..."

"I know, and maybe I'll think about it..."

It was odd, but Julia suddenly felt a little embarrassed by the whole episode and so too, she realised, did Ricky. He followed her to the door and they stood awkwardly just looking at each other for a few moments then Julia took a deep breath and turned away.

Chapter Twelve

By the middle of the following week Julia had fully recovered from the rigours of both her evening at the Regency hotel and the arduous work out that Marsha had put her through.

The welts striping her bottom and thighs had healed quickly, leaving no trace of the whippings she had received, and now, every time she thought back to the events of that hectic evening, she felt herself becoming physically aroused to such an extent that on more than one occasion she was driven to find relief in masturbation.

After careful consideration she had decided not to mention her activities in the down-town gym to Nico or Natalie, fearing that they might disapprove of Marsha taking charge over her at such short notice, and the least she said about Ricky the better.

In any case she herself had mixed feelings about the whole thing. She knew she had been blatantly used by Marsha but she couldn't repress a tingle of excitement each time she remembered how she had lain naked and helpless yet writhing in ecstasy as Ricky had fucked her on the narrow bench.

Every morning Julia worked out for three hours in the local gym. Her body was becoming leaner and firmer. Nico and Natalie continued to be unavailable, leaving her feeling bored and more than a little frustrated. So the call, when it came, made her so excited that she could feel herself becoming flustered, her answers tumbling out in marked contrast to Natalie's calm and efficient tones.

"I'll forward you the details about the weekend and some clothes by messenger first thing tomorrow."

She broke the connection leaving Julia to spend the rest of the day in an agony of anticipation, which was relieved only by the arrival next morning of the messenger who delivered a slim, gift wrapped box. Hands trembling she ripped it open to find a skirt, jacket and shoes together with a terse, typewritten note informing her that she was to be waiting in the street outside her apartment at precisely two o clock that afternoon, wearing the clothes provided.

That meant the clothes provided and nothing else. There was no need to say so. It was always understood.

The skirt was very short indeed. The bolero style jacket left her midriff bare and scarcely concealed the swell of her breasts. The shoes too seemed to accentuate how little she was wearing, the high heels drawing attention to her taut thighs and, as always when scantily and provocatively dressed, she spent long moments in front of the mirror, imagining the effect she would have on a casual observer.

The afternoon air was chilly with the threat of rain and Julia felt herself shivering as she took up position on the pavement outside her apartment block, her clothes offering scant protection against either the cool breeze that explored beyond the bare length of her thighs or the frank stares of passers by, their gazes lingering on her body as she waited. Traffic was heavy but at exactly two o'clock the familiar long limousine with heavily shaded windows drew into the sidewalk and the rear door swung open.

Julia scrambled hastily inside, settling herself on the rear facing jump seat as the car moved smoothly back into the traffic. She could see now that the rear seat proper was occupied by Natalie and two men, both young and both regarding her with undisguised interest. From the cut of their clothes she could tell they were either wealthy or employed in well paid positions, and she wondered vaguely what kind of service they could provide for Nico. Obviously, whatever was planned for her would involve them both and she knew what kind of services she would be required to provide, but for now she concentrated her full attention on Natalie.

"This, gentlemen, is Julia."

Both men nodded and the younger of them leaned forward as though to inspect her more closely.

"Yes, she looks every bit as desirable as I've been led to believe, but isn't she a little overdressed?"

"I agree she can be presented ready for action as it were, but I thought you might appreciate watching the goods being unwrapped. And having her naked on the sidewalk is not very practical."

"You could make her do that if you wished?"

"Oh yes."

Both men chuckled aloud at the idea, but Julia sat still and said nothing. Already she was being treated as a mere object of curiosity and entertainment rather than as a real person with feelings and yet as ever, the very indifference of her companions to her situation seemed to heighten the sense of excitement growing inside her.

"About this unwrapping, then," said one of the men. "Let me see her tits first."

He settled back in the seat as his companion nodded agreement and Natalie snapped her fingers. It was an unnecessary gesture for Julia's hands were already reaching up, fingers working on the buttons of the brief jacket.

"Slowly, Julia. We have a reasonably long drive ahead."

Julia nodded understanding, holding the open halves of the jacket together for a little longer than was necessary before peeling it aside to reveal the proud swell of her breasts. Already she could feel her nipples half erect, the eyes of the two men drawn instantly to them. Carefully she peeled the garment fully away from her body, arching her back as she slipped her arms free, the action thrusting her breasts ever more boldly towards her audience.

Almost tentatively, one of the men reached out for her and Julia sat absolutely still as his fingers brushed across her offered mounds before closing around one hard, swelling nipple.

"Feel her, Bob. She's hot for it already."

Julia blushed at such an obvious comment on her undoubted state of arousal, and moments later the other man reached for her, his hand moulding confidently around her breast, squeezing the firm yet pliant flesh until she was unable to suppress a small shiver.

"Let's see what she's got under that skirt."

Julia flushed again, knowing how they would react to the sight of her stripped utterly naked and knowing too how she herself would react to posing naked in front of them. Already she could feel her nipples swelling harder, the lips of her sex becoming hot and wet at the thought of what she was doing and where such actions would inevitably lead and then her hand went to the fastening of the short skirt, hesitating only briefly before snapping it loose. As with the jacket, she held the garment closed for a few seconds before peeling it aside to reveal the full extent of her nakedness beneath.

"Geez, Mike, she's as smooth as a baby."

Mike needed no telling, his fingers already trailing across the smooth shaven swell of Julia's pubic mound.

"I don't shave that close myself. Bet she has to be real careful!"

Both men laughed aloud and Julia lowered her eyes, waiting for the inevitable order.

"Come on, don't be shy. Open your legs and give us a really good look."

Another burst of laughter echoed around the car and Julia reflected at the sheer unreality of her situation. She was sitting naked in full view of two total strangers and about to expose herself even more lewdly and shamelessly and yet outside the car were normal people, carrying on with their lives, totally unsuspecting of anything out of the ordinary just a few feet away from where they stood. For a few seconds she wondered what would happen if Natalie or either of the two men were to stop the car and order her out onto the sidewalk, and a kind of panic gripped her at the thought of how helpless she was to resist such an order.

"Hey, get those legs apart!"

Bob's voice had an angry edge, dragging her back from her thoughts and she jerked upright.

"I'm sorry. I thought you wanted me to take my time."

"Yeah, well, don't take all day."

Both men chuckled again and Julia breathed a silent sigh of relief as she began slowly to part her thighs. The sight absorbed the eager gaze of both men and Julia forced herself to sit as still as she could, her own eyes fixed on the blacked out rear window, aware of Natalie looking on with a half mocking smile on her lips.

Despite the humiliating treatment, she could feel a pulse of excitement pounding inside her. Her sex peeled wetly open, the lips already puffed up and swollen in open invitation as her thighs parted wider and wider.

She hesitated, and looked at Natalie. What she saw convinced her that she must do whatever they wanted.

Soon she was totally exposed, fully committed to her lewd display, sliding her hands down her belly and opening herself even wider as though defying them to take her where she sat.

"Now let's see the back view."

It was tight and awkward to turn around but Julia struggled into position until she was kneeling, her body bent as far forward over the jump seat as she could manage, her bottom thrust up and out behind her. She was very tense, dreading a touch, and then remained quite still as she felt hands roaming freely across her buttocks, pulling the rounded cheeks apart to further expose the tightly puckered opening.

"She looks real tight to me. Are you sure Nico lets guys fuck her there?"

"Of course. Whatever you want. Actually, she is a tight fuck everywhere. Isn't that so, Julia?"

"Yes, Mistress."

Julia felt her face burning as Natalie discussed her in such coarse terms, the conversation leaving her in no doubt as to what lay in store for her when they finally reached their destination.

"We can fuck her any time we like?"

"Any time and as many times as you like."

"What about whipping her?"

Bob's voice was hoarse with anticipation and Julia felt herself tensing as she waited for Natalie's reply.

"If you want to whip her then that's all right by me but I would suggest a limit of six strokes a time and preferably no more than a dozen a day."

Bob whistled in appreciation and Julia shivered at the prospect of regular floggings over the days ahead, sure that neither man would willingly forgo the excitement of seeing her writhing under the lash or cane.

"Get up now. We'll be arriving soon."

Julia scrambled back onto the seat, careful under Natalie's watchful eye to keep her legs parted as before. She could see now that they had left the city behind. The country road along which they were travelling was lined with trees and almost free of other traffic. Both men were sitting comfortably back and gazing intently at her, the wicked gleam in their eyes and the very obvious bulges at their crotches testifying to their growing sense of excitement.

"You might also wish to restrain her, gentlemen. I believe you might find it arousing."

Natalie fished about in her pocket for a few moments and brought out a short length of twisted up chain which she laid out on her lap and began to untangle.

"You're familiar with these of course, Julia?"

Julia nodded, recognising the two nipple clips. They were attached to each end of the chain and there was a separate ring set in the middle, very obviously designed to tether the wearer in place. The chain itself looked fairly substantial and she wondered about the weight of it dragging at her nipples. She licked her lips, leaning forward without being told. Her breasts swung outwards, the nipples already more than half erect and Natalie turned briefly to her companions.

"I need Julia's nipples really hard... would you oblige?"

Without hesitation both men reached out for her, fingers closing around her swelling nipples, pulling and teasing the tender buds. She felt herself responding at once, breasts tingling and quivering under the persistent stimulation, small shocks of pleasure rippling through her. Without conscious thought she leaned further forward, offering herself shamelessly, her breath quickening and her thighs parting wider to reveal her growing arousal.

Bob reached for her, his hand slipping quickly up the inside of her open thighs, brushing right up against her sex and sending a shudder of urgent need pulsing through her.

"Enough for now," said Natalie. "There will be plenty of time later for whatever you want."

With obvious reluctance both men sank back into their seats and Julia choked back a low moan of frustration. Natalie had untangled the chain and she picked up one of the circular clips, nipping the small tabs between her finger and thumb to open the ring fully. Her free hand reached for Julia's swaying breasts, fingers closing around one hard, thrusting nipple, pulling steadily and persistently until Julia moaned softly and then the ring was slipped around the jutting bud of flesh and both tabs released, allowing the ring to close firmly in place.

The second ring followed at once and now Julia's nipples looked swollen to bursting point as they strained out from the tight confines of the encircling rings. Between her breasts the chain hung in a shallow arc, the weight dragging at her trapped flesh and sending throbbing shocks of pain rippling through her at the slightest movement.

Both Mike and Bob were gaping at her openly, unable to fully take in her ready submission. Julia knew that once she was left alone with the pair of them, any inhibitions would soon disappear and they would want to exert their power over her again and again in the manner now being demonstrated by Natalie.

Now she found the very helplessness of her plight arousing to the exclusion of all other feelings, revelling in the excited interest she was attracting from the two men. Natalie was reaching for her again, a slender leash dangling from her hand, but Julia didn't even bother to look down as she felt her chain lifted and the leash snapped into place around the central ring.

"I think you'll agree, gentlemen that Julia will now follow you anywhere with the minimum of fuss."

"I just bet she will."

Mike laughed out loud, his gaze locked onto her jutting nipples and Julia braced herself for his touch but there was no time.

The car turned off the highway, easing along a narrow tree lined lane, and a few minutes later there was the crunch of gravel beneath the wheels as it passed under a stone archway and into the drive of a substantial hunting lodge.

"We're here."

The announcement was unnecessary but Julia could

appreciate the excitement that Bob and Mike were feeling. In truth she too had felt a surge of excited anticipation the moment the car had left the highway, knowing that soon, very soon, Natalie would further demonstrate her authority by whipping her.

Chapter Thirteen

The car doors opened and both Bob and Mike climbed out at once. Cool air spilled into the warm interior and Julia shivered, her nipples hardening within their constraining rings as she waited for Natalie to take up the leash and parade her naked in front of the waiting men.

Through the open doors she could see members of the household staff advancing towards the car and she realised at once that Natalie intended to make her humiliation complete by parading her in front of them all. Natalie was watching her, the end of the leash dangling loosely in her hand.

"Showtime, Julia."

Julia reflected that both Bob and Mike had already been treated to an eyeful of what she had to offer but she squared her shoulders, thrusting her breasts almost defiantly forward as she followed Natalie from the car. Outside, the gravel drive was sharp underfoot and as the full chill of the late afternoon hit her she shivered, her nipples at once tightening and throbbing almost painfully.

The staff unloading luggage from the car regarded her with frank and open curiosity, their eyes flicking over her nude body and lingering on the smooth shaven mound of her sex. The fact that she was tethered to the leash by her nipples caused several of them to stare openly in disbelief until despite the cold she felt herself flushing hot with embarrassment.

The door to the lodge was open and inviting and she wished Natalie would hurry up and lead her inside instead of lingering on the drive. But her humiliation was far from over. Mike approached her, obviously fascinated both by the manner in which she was tethered and by the way her nipples were reacting to the cool air. He reached out and fondled her breasts, making sure that the household staff had a clear view of what he was doing to her and Julia blushed an even deeper shade of red.

"How about whipping her now, Natalie?"

His voice was low, excited, his hands cupping Julia's breasts while Natalie pretended to consider her reply.

"If that's what you want."

"That's what we want! Right, Bob?"

Bob nodded agreement, his own expression excited at the prospect, and Natalie began to lead Julia towards the house.

"No outside. We want to see her whipped right here in the open."

Julia's jaw dropped in amazement and she looked desperately at Natalie, dismayed to see that the young girl was pondering the request.

"Well... I don't see why not."

"Yeah, it'll warm her up too. She looks a little cold right now."

Both men laughed out loud and Julia opened her mouth to protest.

"Do you want to say something, Julia?"

Julia shook her head. Any protest would be to no avail and might even carry a risk of increased punishment. She could see the staff pricking up their ears before hurrying back to the house with the luggage. No doubt by the time the whipping began she would have an eager audience at every window. The thought both filled her with dread and yet at the same time stirred feelings of excitement deep inside her.

Both Mike and Bob crowded in close to her, their eyes wide and eager. Natalie was casting about for a suitable spot and at last she settled on a tall sapling, one of a number of young trees planted along the edge of the drive. The trunk of the tree was straight and still quite thin, the bark smooth and even. More importantly, it was situated almost immediately in front of the lodge, affording anyone watching from the windows a perfectly clear view.

Julia was led across to stand in front of the tree, Bob and Mike following so close behind her that she could almost feel their mounting excitement.

Natalie pondered for a few moments, taking measurements by eye, and then she reached for Julia's breasts, unclipping one of the nipple rings. There was a wicked gleam in her eye as she urged Julia closer to the tree until she was standing pressed right up against it.

The bark felt cold against her skin, as Natalie pushed her closer, making sure that her breasts were pushed out to either side of the slender trunk. Julia realised what she intended but before she had time to struggle she felt a firm hand pressed into her back holding her in place. Whether it was Mike or Bob holding her she neither knew nor cared, her wide eyed gaze fixed on Natalie as the young girl passed the loose end of the chain on her nipple rings around the back of the tree and clipped the ring back around her still hard and jutting nipple, chaining her to the tree by her breasts.

The two men behind her murmured their approval at such a novel method of restraint but Natalie was not quite finished.

"Raise your arms up over your head."

Julia obeyed. The action lifted her breasts so that they thrust out from her body even more boldly. Natalie nodded in approval, then seized her wrists and placed them on either side of the tree trunk before reaching for the long leather leash still attached to her nipple rings. It was the work of only a few moments to wrap the leash securely around Julia's wrists, knotting it tight and binding her even more firmly in place.

Natalie nodded slightly and the hands pressing Julia hard against the tree were removed. It made little difference to her situation for the chain between her nipples was stretched so tight around the tree trunk that she had no room for movement. The leash was also stretched tight up to her wrists, exerting a steady upward pull on her breasts. She was held in place by her wrists and her nipples, the slim trunk of the tree passing between her breasts and rubbing up against her belly. Any movement at all was difficult and painful and yet she knew that she would not be able to prevent herself writhing and twisting under the sting of the lash.

Already she felt a dull, throbbing ache in her breasts and the cool air caused her to shiver as she waited quietly for the beating to begin. It would not begin just yet, she knew, for Natalie delighted in making her wait, prolonging the tension and increasing her own pleasure.

She concentrated on breathing deeply and evenly, doing her best to ignore the cold that seemed to seep into her, sapping her resistance. Behind her back she could sense the household staff gathering at the windows to watch her ordeal. She could imagine the coarse comments passing between them and was suddenly thankful that Natalie had positioned her facing away from the house so she did not have to see them all looking at her.

There was no avoiding Bob and Mike, both of them circling her slowly, feasting their eyes on her tethered, straining breasts, reaching out repeatedly to fondle her as she stood helpless. At first it was just her breasts, their fingers circling and tugging at her nipples until they swelled even harder, straining out from the confines of the rings. She couldn't suppress her gasps and moans under the relentless teasing. Next they moved round behind her, their hands roaming freely over the taut curves of her backside.

"Nice firm ass. I'm really looking forward to watching it jiggle about when Natalie whips her."

"Yeah. You think maybe she'll let us whip her instead?"

Julia tensed as they considered the possibility, knowing that sooner or later she would have to submit to them but fervently hoping that it would not be now, with everyone watching. She knew from painful experience that the presence of an audience, however small, always spurred whoever was whipping her to lay on the strokes with greater ferocity as though to demonstrate their total power over her.

"We'll ask her when she gets back."

Mike nodded, squeezing Julia's buttocks hard, his fingers digging sharply into her. In response to their brusque commands she parted her thighs wider, rising up onto her toes to relieve the persistent upward pull on her breasts, fingers at once probed deep between her legs and prised the cheeks of her bottom apart, exposing the dark puckered opening nestling deep inside her crease and delved down to stroke insistently along the soft furrow of her sex.

She was already aroused from the attention they had paid to her breasts, the lips of her sex hot and damp, inviting penetration. Under the insistent, lewd fondling they grew hotter and wetter, gaping open between her parted thighs while she gasped and shuddered, her arousal growing with each passing minute.

Despite the chill a sheen of perspiration glistened on her breasts, her breathing becoming shallow and ragged as her body responded to the relentless stimulation. She knew she was being shamelessly manipulated but bound as she was there was no way to resist.

She shuddered again and suddenly she didn't want to resist any more. Her legs trembled and she moaned softly, pushing herself down onto the fingers thrusting so wantonly between her thighs. She didn't care that the lewd tableau was being played out for the amusement of the men fondling her and the cheap entertainment of the staff watching from the house. All that mattered were the fingers lingering along the lips of her sex. She wanted them inside her, stretching her wide while she surrendered herself to the pleasure rippling through her.

"Hot little bitch, isn't she?"

Julia moaned aloud in frustration at the sound of Natalie's voice. At once both Bob and Mike stepped back and she almost sobbed aloud as she was left hanging, her body hot and alive with arousal. No doubt Natalie had been watching them quietly for some time, waiting until she was trembling on the brink of release before announcing her presence. Mike began to stammer out an embarrassed reply but Natalie waved him to silence.

"Don't worry about it, that's what we brought her here for, isn't it?"

Mike brightened up at once and Julia's spirits sank as she remembered that both he and Bob had talked about wanting to whip her themselves. It appeared that Natalie too had overheard the conversation.

"I suppose you'd like to whip her now?"

"Yeah! Right!"

Their voices were breathless with excitement and Julia sagged against the tree at the prospect of a savage thrashing. Behind her she could hear the two men tossing a coin to decide who should have the pleasure of wielding the whip first. She could have turned her head to watch but it made no difference. Either one would be seeking to outdo the other and she concentrated on bracing herself against the coming onslaught.

Bob shouted with delight as he won the toss and at Natalie's suggestion he walked around the tree to show Julia the whip. It was a horsewhip, three feet of shiny, braided leather swaying stiffly from a thick handled grip and Julia sucked in her breath. Bob was holding it firmly, brandishing it triumphantly in front of her, his eyes shining.

"Guess this will really make you jump."

Julia said nothing, her mouth very dry as she pondered the searing imprint the lash would leave across her tender behind. It certainly would make her jump and she pressed herself harder against the tree, very mindful of the chain tethering her nipples. He moved out of sight behind her and Julia flinched as she felt Natalie's hand on her bottom.

"I suggest you whip her between here and here and I'm sure you'll find she's very responsive just about here."

Natalie brushed her hand over Julia's jutting behind, lingering on the softer flesh where the full swell of her buttocks flowed down into her thighs. The hand was removed and Julia pressed herself even harder against the tree, sucking in her breath as she waited for the first stinging stroke. She didn't have long to wait.

Swish!

Whack!

The first blow cracked full across her defenceless backside almost as soon as Natalie's hand was clear. The pain was intense, a blaze of heat that ripped through her and drew an anguished gasp from her clamped lips. She jerked hard up against her bonds, back arched, buttocks quivering.

Swish!

Thwack!

The second blow whistled in, slashing a burning diagonal stripe across her backside, the pain more intense where it cut across the first still reddening weal. The chain rattled against the tree and Julia felt a sharp tug at her nipples but she was powerless to control the desperate twisting of her body under the savage thrashing.

Swish!

Whack!

A third time the wicked leather cracked down, cutting another searing diagonal across her taut behind, criss crossing the two welts already stinging her and dragging a long wail of distress from her. Three strokes only and her entire backside was on fire. The rings clamped around her nipples pulled at her painfully and she clutched at the tree with her bound hands, desperate to control the wild thrusting and jerking of her hips, She had been right in guessing that Bob would lay into her as hard as he could and now Mike would be eager to show that he could do just as well if not better.

She hung, gasping and helpless, her body suddenly hot and dripping with sweat, her heart pounding as she waited for the renewed onslaught.

Swish!

Crack!

This time she howled aloud, her back arching sharply until the chain tethering her pulled her up short. Her backside blazed and she realised that Mike had laid his first blow exactly alongside the first weal laid into her by Bob, cutting across the two stripes criss crossing her behind. She twisted her head, eyes wet and pleading but there was no respite.

Swish!

Thwack!

Another diagonal stripe and this time it intersected three burning weals. She writhed helplessly in her bonds, heedless of the savage pull on her nipples, her bottom jerking and quivering beyond control.

One more to make six. Only one more savage stroke and it would be over. Or would it? She gritted her teeth, tasting the salty tang of the tears trickling down her cheeks. Just one more stinging stroke. She could take it. She had to!

Swish!

Crack!

It fell with an almost savage ferocity, criss crossing her backside and cutting across every welt that still seared and stung her, the sudden fiery pain slamming her hard up against the tree and driving the breath from her body in one explosive gasp. Her hands gripped the tree as her body shuddered and shook, her breasts heaving as she struggled to keep herself from breaking down completely.

Then it seemed to be over!

She sagged limply, sobbing with relief.

Her backside was on fire and her body trembled. Incredibly, she was still physically aroused, the lips of her sex still wet and open between her legs.

As the mist of pain cleared from her eyes the feelings of desire and need that had gripped her before the thrashing now crept irresistibly back through her body. She shuddered gently in her bonds. The heat of the thrashing flared up into her belly, and she shuddered again as a familiar feeling of lust swept through her.

She would be fucked soon. She always was after a thrashing. She could hear the two men close behind her, their own breathing quick and ragged as they watched her. They would be excited and worked up by the beating they had given her and by the sight and sound of her helpless struggles. She could imagine them clearly, faces flushed, erections straining.

She wondered if they would just untie her and fuck her openly right there in front of the house or take her inside. It didn't really matter. All that mattered was submitting to them and pleasing them. The sensuous feel of an erect cock thrusting hard up into her would be enough to make her forget the dreadful stinging in her backside.

She suddenly longed to be taken down and used, uncaring of how many of the staff were watching. Without thinking, she whimpered softly, pressing herself against the tree, its bark cool across her heated skin.

"Think she's all right?"

Mike sounded uncertain but Natalie hastened to reassure him.

"Of course she is. She's always like this after a good thrashing."

He reached out for her, fingers trailing along the vivid red welts striping her behind. She gasped out loud, stiffening against the rekindled sting where he touched her, another low whimper escaping from her lips.

"Maybe we overdid it a little?"

"No, I don't think so. But why not leave her to recover for a while?"

"Yeah, right. I could do with a drink anyway."

Bob murmured agreement and to Julia's horror they turned away from her towards the warmth and comfort of the house.

"See you later, Julia. Don't go away now."

Their laughter echoed in her ears and Julia sagged limply in despair. She wanted to call them back, plead with them to release her, but was struck dumb by the sense of unfairness of it all. First they had thrashed her publicly and now they intended to leave her strung up on display like some cheap trophy, the evidence of the thrashing plain for all to see. It was so unfair but there was nothing she could do.

Chapter Fourteen

Julia's whole body ached.

Her arms were numb and her breasts throbbed painfully both from the tightly constraining rings clipped around her nipples and the chill of the late afternoon air. She shivered repeatedly as the chill pervaded her body, thankful only that the cold had succeeded in reducing the hot stinging in her backside to a dull, throbbing ache.

Around her, the shadows were lengthening as the sun went down and she wondered if Natalie intended leaving her tethered and on display until it was too dark for anyone from the house to see her. If she twisted her head around she would be able to see the house, windows shining with light and the promise of warmth, but she resisted the temptation. Along with warmth, the house held the certainty of yet more abuse.

The shadows lengthened further and she shivered again. The chain binding her to the tree tugged against her nipples with the movement. The metal felt very cold and hard around her tender flesh and she hoped she would not have to endure the bondage for much longer.

Then at last she heard something and twisted her head awkwardly around. She almost cried out with relief as she saw someone walking across the drive towards her.

In the half light she wasn't sure if it was a man or a woman, but the sight represented freedom and she offered up a sigh of thanks. It was a man, dressed in the uniform of a butler although he looked so thin and cadaverous that she was sure he could be mistaken for a funeral director. There was something altogether sinister about him.

He took his time, standing back to inspect her closely before beginning to untie her. First he reached up to unfasten her wrists and Julia brought her arms gratefully down to her sides, sighing once more as the cramps racking her were relieved. His hands dropped down to her tethered breasts, hesitating slightly, and she could see the gleam in his eyes as he wrestled with the temptation to fondle her. She knew he would for she was positioned to face away from the house, her body shielding him from view and she braced herself for the first touch of his fingers.

His hands were like claws and she flinched as his fingers traced a slow path around her breasts, forcing herself to remain still as he fondled her. He pinched her trapped nipples and she sucked in her breath, feeling her legs beginning to tremble.

His eyes gleamed in the half light as he continued stroking and pulling at the tender buds until she could restrain her feelings no longer and shuddered openly.

"Ohhh, please, please don't."

"You like it, don't you?"

"Yes, yes, but you mustn't..."

She was gasping, her frustration boiling up inside her at the relentless stimulation, and he grinned at the response he had teased from her. Under the cover of her body, he slipped one hand around the tree, groping for her sex.

"No... please..."

Her voice was urgent, fearing what would happen if they were observed, knowing that Natalie would seize on the opportunity of blaming her for wanton behaviour with the servants despite her helpless situation. The man ignored her, his fingers working down her belly, finding the open and inviting slit of her sex and slipping quickly inside.

She sucked in her breath again, struggling to control the trembling in her legs as he fingered her, stretching her wider as he worked his fingers deeper inside. Already she could feel herself becoming wet, her sex lips hot and gaping despite the chill pervading the rest of her body.

"They're going to fuck you when I get you back inside.."

His fingers were making soft sucking noises as they slipped wetly in and out of her now burning sex.

"I wonder if they'll let me watch."

The reminder that she was soon to be fucked and the thought that this man using her so casually might be allowed to watch sent a wave of perverse excitement rippling through her. His fingers were relentless, insistent and she shuddered openly, suddenly wanting him to make her climax but fearful of the consequences. He saw the conflicting emotions on her face and chuckled.

"They won't of course, so maybe I'd better just make the most of you now."

He thrust his fingers deeper, burrowing into the hot, wet pit of her belly until she quivered all over, panting on the brink of release.

"No... please... you mustn't!"

"Unfortunately they're waiting for you inside."

His fingers slipped easily out of her and he wiped them dry on her belly before returning to the task of freeing her from her bonds.

"Mind you, girl, given just half a chance I'll have more than my fingers stuffed up that tight little slit of yours."

His chuckle was low and coarse and Julia sagged limply, her body flooded with a confusion of arousal and relief. Her nipples strained out from the rings and as the butler reached for them she moaned aloud, flinching at the touch of his fingers against the sensitive buds.

"Like the feel of that, do you?"

Julia moaned again as he squeezed her hard, his fingers sending sharp jolts of mingled pain and pleasure through her breasts.

"I'll have my hands around these a few more times too, just see if I don't."

Chuckling to himself as he worked, he closed his fingers around the tabs of the nipple rings, nipping them open and pulling them free. Julia staggered back, gasping out loud at the strong tingling sensation that flooded through her breasts as the pressure around her nipples was suddenly released. The temptation to reach up and cradle her abused breasts was tremendous but she fought against it, waiting quietly as the butler gathered up the chain and the leash.

"Walk in front so I can get a real good look."

She turned around, presenting him with a view of her well thrashed behind and he chuckled again.

"They made a real mess of your backside!"

She half turned towards him, her voice low and hesitant.

"Did they... am I bleeding?"

He chuckled again, shaking his head and relief flooded through her.

"No, they didn't cut you at all but I'm surprised they didn't the way they were both laying into you."

He grinned again, noting her flush of embarrassment.

"Real good entertainment it was, watching you jump around, maybe they'll do it again. What do you think?"

Julia had no doubt that both Bob and Mike would want to do it again, probably quite soon.

"I-I really don't know."

"A real odd ball you are, girl. Still, whatever turns you on I suppose. Sure turned me on watching you though."

He motioned her towards the house and Julia trudged carefully across the drive, the gravel sharp under her feet once more. She could see faces crowding at the windows to watch her but she didn't care. All that mattered and what was now uppermost in her thoughts was that Bob and Mike were waiting for her.

Natalie would be waiting too and she was sure the young girl would claim her for the night, but for now she would be required to satisfy the demands of the two men who had been brought here with her. She was going to be fucked very soon whether she wanted it or not, and the butler following close behind knew it too, along with everyone else in the house.

She wondered if she would be fucked just as she had been whipped, in full view of anyone who cared to watch. She was surprised to find she didn't really care. All that mattered was that the frustration still boiling deep inside her would soon be relieved and without conscious thought she quickened her pace towards the open door of the lodge.

Chapter Fifteen

The two days that followed were more than enough to satisfy the butler's evil desires.

The two men insisted that their victim remain naked at all times. As they were both young and virile, scarcely an hour went by without Julia finding herself being enthusiastically fucked by either one or the other.

In between times and whenever she was inside the house, it seemed she only had to turn around to find the butler lurking nearby, ever ready to make a grab for her breasts or thrust his hand insolently down between her legs whenever he was sure they could not be observed.

As he had taken every opportunity to find excuses for entering a room where he knew either Bob or Mike would be fucking or beating her and had not been rebuked for his behaviour, she was unsure whether or not a blind eye was being turned to the liberties he was constantly taking with her.

Natalie certainly seemed disinterested, spending much of her time working in her bedroom, and Julia did not dare to complain.

All the same, she loathed the man and took great pains to avoid him, even pushing him away quite roughly when he managed on one heart stopping occasion to pin her against the kitchen door.

Both Bob and Mike seemed aware of her problems but seemed equally disinclined to step in on her behalf and she had no intention of raising the matter with them, fearful that they would see the whole thing as a joke and actively encourage the man.

They might even invite him to fuck her while they watched!

Fortunately, there turned out to be more to the weekend than non stop sex.

The house itself was actually a hunting lodge, set in several acres of prime hunting land together with a small lake for fishing, and it was with some relief that Julia discovered Bob and Mike to be keen sportsmen.

Immediately after breakfast they set off for either the woods or the lake, returning only for lunch before setting off on their sporting pursuits once more and staying out until early evening.

Julia had to accompany them, and she had mixed feelings on the matter. It enabled her to escape from the unwelcome attentions of the butler, but she was often cold and the fact that she was naked and in the open seemed to unearth some primitive desires in her companions.

She lost count of the number of fallen trees she had been tied to, spread-eagled either face down or face up while the two men took it in turns to beat her.

Other times they tied her wrists to high branches, keeping her body stretched taut for what seemed like hours while they fished or hunted, returning to her at frequent intervals to toy with her breasts and sex until she was panting with arousal.

Sometimes they fucked her there and then but at other times they seemed to find great amusement in just leaving her hanging and frustrated.

When they whipped her out in the open, it was not with the horsewhip but with slender leather straps. Somehow the leather seemed to sting much more when it cracked down across flesh that was chilled through and she couldn't prevent herself crying out loudly as each stroke whipped in, again much to their amusement.

Both men loved it, revelling in the power and control they exercised over her.

As she had known and feared, each wanted to outdo the other and however vivid and sore the welts already striping her backside, they showed her no mercy, meting out a full half dozen stokes each while her cries echoed through the woods or across the lake.

Despite such treatment, or more probably because of it, she passed the whole time at the lodge in a state of more or less constant arousal, relieved only at night when both Bob and Mike drank lots of beer before collapsing into bed, exhausted from the fresh air, exercise and sex.

Natalie claimed her then for a few hours before she too was free to sleep... except that the door of her room had no key against the threat of the butler prowling around in the night.

By late afternoon on Sunday she was totally exhausted. Although bags had been packed, no one appeared in any hurry to leave. Just as it was getting dark, Natalie was called to the telephone, returning after a few minutes in an apologetic mood.

"A slight change of plans, gentlemen."

"Oh, how slight?"

"Well... I know I indicated that Julia would be free to spend the night with both of you once we got back to town but it seems my brother has made alternative arrangements."

"You mean we can't have her?"

Natalie shrugged apologetically.

"The party concerned is very important to our future plans and I include both of you in that statement."

Natalie paused pointedly and Mike nodded in understanding.

"So we don't rock the boat, right?"

"I'm glad you see it that way and I'll certainly make it up to you as soon as I can. In the meantime you have about two hours before the car arrives to collect Julia so I suggest you make the most of them."

She smiled sweetly before turning and walking out of the room, leaving Julia suddenly anxious and confused.

The weekend had been exhausting enough and she had half expected the two men to keep her with them overnight but this was a totally unexpected development.

Worse from her point of view was that it seemed to have caught Natalie by surprise too and yet there was no suggestion of her not being made available.

The two men were obviously determined not to waste a minute of the time that was left. She had been allowed to dress but now Bob eagerly stripped her. She was made to bend over the back of a chair, spreading her legs wide and reaching down to grip the seat.

But that wasn't enough to please them.

"Not like that - get yourself open wide."

Heat rushed to her face as she reached round behind her, pressing her hands to her buttocks and spreading the cheeks wider until the whole of her sex and backside were lewdly exposed.

For the whole of the two hours she stood like that and not since her time in prison had she experienced so much sexual activity in such a short space of time.

Tired though they were, they each managed to fuck her twice, taking her in both her sex and her backside and between times they stood arrogantly in front of her demanding that she both lick them clean and suck on their cocks until they were fully erect once more.

They repeatedly fondled her breasts and when she was not actually being penetrated by either of their rampant cocks, their fingers were thrust deep into her sex, keeping her hot and fully aroused.

Very early in the proceedings the butler had sidled into the room, grinning broadly at the lewd spectacle she presented as she squirmed and shuddered, gasping and panting under the relentless stimulation.

Orgasm after orgasm gripped her perspiring body, her breasts swinging wildly in time with the eager thrusts of the cock penetrating her, her moans and gasps stifled by the cock jammed between her lips.

She was trembling on the verge of exhaustion, sustained only by the orgasmic spasms washing through her over and over again.

She ached all over from the strain of remaining bent across the chair and after only an hour her breasts were tender and throbbing from the constant fondling but still her body responded to each new assault.

At last and as though from a long way off she heard Mike gasping that he was finished with her and telling her to rise.

Bob lay sprawled on the sofa, his eyes closed and she wished she could join him as she pushed herself painfully upright. She guessed that she looked a mess, her face flushed red, her body shining with sweat and sticky trails of sperm seeping from her sex and backside.

"The car's here."

"I need to wash."

She turned hesitantly towards the door where Natalie stood waiting.

"I don't think it matters, Julia. You can get cleaned up when we get there."

Julia longed to know more about where she was going but knew that she wouldn't get an answer.

Perhaps even Natalie herself didn't know.

She walked out into the night on trembling legs and into the back of the waiting car without another word.

"Remember, Julia, these people are important to us."

She nodded vaguely to Natalie as the door closed and as the car sped away she was already asleep.

How long the journey took she had no idea, only half waking as she was helped from the car on arrival.

The car was parked alongside a darkened building and she offered no resistance as the driver took her arm and guided her inside.

The sudden glare of a light snapping on blinded her and she stumbled forward, almost falling over a low bed.

"Lie down."

The driver helped her, laying her flat on her back, the light glaring down into her eyes so she could hardly see.

"Now don't give me any trouble."

She was too tired to either resist or care as first her ankles and then her wrists were secured to the bedframe.

"Someone will come for you in the morning."

Without another word the driver left, switching off the light behind him and plunging the room into darkness.

Moments later she heard a key turning in the lock and she sank weakly back on the bed.

Wherever she was and whoever had sent for her she was a prisoner for now and quite helpless to do anything about it. She closed her eyes and moments later was once more fast asleep.

Chapter Sixteen

In the early morning light and from what she could see whilst tied down, Julia discovered that she was locked in a barred cage which itself stood in one corner of a large, almost square room, sparsely furnished with a small table and a number of chairs.

The walls of the room were painted an even white and had narrow windows set high up in two walls through which sunlight was streaming, giving the place a light and airy feel.

She twisted her head further around and discovered that her cage contained a toilet and a shower fitting, exactly like the cell she had occupied in prison so many months ago, and she guessed that she was destined to spend many hours behind the bars.

On the wall outside the cage, out of reach but directly in sight, was a long rack from which hung an equally familiar assortment of whips and canes. She turned her gaze up to the ceiling and was not at all surprised to see a fearsome arrangement of chains and manacles hanging down.

The design of the cage puzzled her, for instead of an unbroken run of steel bars from floor to ceiling, there was a pattern of linked circles running around the whole width at a height of about four to five feet from the ground. They were certainly not there for pure decorative effect!

Her musings were interrupted by the entry of a maid, and she guessed that in addition to everything else she was under the survey of a concealed camera and her awakening had been observed.

She knew the drill well and was not surprised at all to find that the maid had brought shaving implements as well as breakfast. Once freed from her shackles she made use of the toilet and then went directly to the shower without any instruction being necessary, soaping herself for a full five minutes under the freezing spray before bending to the task of shaving her pubic mound silky smooth.

Only then, after carefully inspecting her work, did the maid speak, informing her curtly that she was to finish breakfast within fifteen minutes after which she would be suitably prepared for her new mistress to see her.

So she was to entertain another woman with all that implied. Julia felt her heartbeat quicken with a kind of dreadful anticipation as she hurried to gulp down the meal, wary of giving any cause for offence yet strangely eager to discover who it was who now laid claim to her.

Almost to the minute the maid returned and removed the tray before beckoning Julia to stand close up against the bars of the cage.

Close to, Julia could see that the pattern of rings about which she had pondered were set at roughly the level of her breasts and the dawning certainty as to their purpose was confirmed as the maid measured her up by eye and bent to adjust the height of a narrow step which Julia could now see running along the base of the cage.

Once it was adjusted and locked in place the maid stood back and without needing to be told Julia stepped up onto the narrow ledge and reached out to grab hold of the bars to steady herself.

Moving quickly now, the maid went to the rack on the wall, returning with an assortment of leather straps with which she proceeded to fasten Julia's wrists and ankles to the bars, securing her firmly with her arms and legs spread wide in the shape of a cross.

Wider straps were then passed around her waist and

under her arms, fastening her even more tightly against the bars. As those straps were cinched tight she could feel the firm mounds of her breasts being squeezed inexorably through two of the rings.

The metal felt cold as it slid across the softness of her skin and her nipples began to swell almost at once in response, throbbing insistently as she was finally secured hard up against the bars, spread and helpless and ready to receive her mistress.

The maid collected the breakfast tray and left her alone with her thoughts. Julia longed to know how long she must wait and what was to be required of her, but it would be useless to ask and a feeling of uneasiness began to creep over her.

Many times over the past weeks she had stood naked and bound, unable to touch her own breasts while those same breasts were freely available to be touched by whoever desired them, but never before had she felt so vulnerable as she did now, her body effectively divided in two by the bars of the cage. The rings fitted snugly around her but not so tight as to constrict her painfully. Squinting down, she could just see each firm hemisphere jutting proudly out, nipples now fully hard and swollen. A tremor rippled through her as she imagined how she must look to whoever came into the room, her body so openly and invitingly on show.

As always in such situations, time seemed to drag by, her apprehension growing with each passing minute, until with a genuine sense of relief she saw the door open and her heart began to pound madly as she strained to catch sight of her mistress.

It was Marsha, the woman who had looked on so dispassionately while Julia had exercised to the point of exhaustion for her entertainment and who had later whipped her so intimately and she felt a shudder of very real fear run through her at the thought of being so thoroughly in the clutches of such a cool and calculating woman.

"Well, Julia, I said we would meet again and here we are, just the two of us."

Julia said nothing, watching carefully as Marsha closed the door behind her and made her way slowly across the room. She envied the other woman her poise and elegance while she in contrast hung naked and exposed from the bars of the cage.

Marsha's skin glowed from recent exercise. A short tennis dress hugged the firm curves of her body, emphasising her shapely figure, and Julia felt her spirits sinking at the prospect of endless punishing work-outs under the supervision of such a fanatic.

"Aren't you pleased to see me, Julia?"

"Oh... yes... very pleased, Mistress."

Julia despised herself for grovelling but worse still was her fear of giving offence.

"You're lying of course, but no matter, I'm very pleased to see you - and so prettily displayed, too."

Marsha halted a few steps away, a mocking smile on her lips as she swept her gaze lingeringly over Julia's body.

"What do you think of my little playroom?"

She swept her hand around to encompass all of the apparatus, her face flushed with a kind of proud excitement.

"I haven't used it for a while but since meeting you I think I should catch up on lost time, don't you agree?"

Julia said nothing but her heart was beginning to beat faster at the memory of her last encounter with this woman and the anxious prospect of spending yet more time alone with her in this room.

Marsha smiled at the sight of her obvious nervousness and moved in closer, reaching round Julia's tightly bound body until she could grip the firm swell of her buttocks.

Julia winced as her fingers dug in, sending sharp stabs

of pain lancing through her still tender flesh.

"Been spending time with men again, Julia?"

"Y-yes."

Julia's body stiffened against the bars as Marsha traced along the raised and still sore weals criss crossing her behind.

"Gave you a real thrashing, did they?"

"Ahhhhh... yes."

The sharp pain stabbed through her again as Marsha pinched her several times and tears sprang to her eyes. She desperately wanted to twist and squirm away from the cruel stimulation, but bound as tightly as she was, could only hang helplessly, her body quivering as Marsha continued the slow, tormenting path across her abused flesh.

"How very crude they were, Julia. Your backside must look like a map of a railroad junction."

Shaking her head, Marsha at last withdrew the hand and Julia almost sobbed aloud with relief.

"I can promise there will be none of that sort of treatment while you're here with me, Julia."

"Thank you, Mistress."

Julia was under no illusions that Marsha would give her an easy time, but she was also aware that a little grovelling could go a long way.

In any case, she was hardly in any position to do anything other than endure whatever lay in store for her with as much fortitude as she could muster.

Marsha smiled at her submission and then became instantly businesslike again.

"You've already sampled a few of my preferences of course and I'm sure you're looking forward to sampling a few more over the next few days. These for example."

Reaching forward, Marsha trailed her hands lightly around the confined curves of Julia's breasts, smiling again as she felt her captive shiver in response.

"So well formed and so sensitive too. Has anyone ever whipped your breasts?"

"No! Oh no!"

Julia was shocked at the suggestion, horribly certain that Marsha intended to do just that. She suddenly realised fully why she had been secured as she was, sure that had she been free she would have resisted and fought against her no matter what the consequences.

"It needs a woman's touch of course, but by the time you leave here you'll be offering these up to me freely on demand."

Julia felt frantic at the prospect of what she was to endure, the more so as she was so tightly secured in position and so helpless to resist or protect herself, but her anguished pleas fell on deaf ears. Marsha crossed over to the rack, running her fingers reflectively over the collection of whips hanging there before making her choice.

"This one should do very nicely. I don't want to do serious damage."

Forcing herself to look at the short six thonged whip, Julia wasn't convinced.

The thongs were slender and supple, knotted at intervals and gathered together at one end to form a secure grip. It hissed loudly through the air as Marsha took a few practice swings.

As if on cue the maid re-entered the room carrying a small bottle and Marsha nodded to her briefly.

"Very good, Harriet, make sure she's well oiled."

Without a word and with no show of emotion whatsoever, Harriet uncorked the bottle and poured a generous quantity of the lightly scented oil across Julia's proffered breasts before proceeding to rub it well into her skin, making sure that not an inch was left uncovered.

Despite her apprehension, Julia couldn't help responding to the gentle stimulation as the maid worked the oil carefully around and across her nipples. Behind her, Marsha continued her practice swings with the whip, obviously amused at Julia's conflicting emotions.

"The oil will make the whip sting a little harder, Julia, but it won't mark you so deeply or for so long.."

Julia could only moan softly in reply, her belly churning in a confusion of fear and arousal as the maid continued the slow oiling of her breasts until at last she withdrew her caressing fingers and left her to hang, gasping and quivering, to face her tormentor.

Marsha was smiling broadly as the maid withdrew, savouring Julia's helplessness and the impending pleasure she would derive from thrashing her so cruelly.

"Six lashes to begin with, three each side. Then we'll take it from there."

Julia shuddered in despair, closing her eyes against the expected onslaught. But even that small relief was to be denied her.

"Open your eyes, girl! I want you to watch."

Trembling, Julia opened her eyes, her gaze drawn immediately to the whip swinging casually in Marsha's grasp as the woman took up position in front of her. Her mouth was suddenly dry and she was very aware of her nipples, still swollen and throbbing, jutting out towards the woman, perfect targets for the lash.

Hisss!

Whack!

In one smooth swift movement Marsha swept the whip across the thrusting swell of Julia's left breast, the slender thongs spreading out in a wide arc, each one searing a stinging path across her tender flesh, the sudden jolt of pain stiffening her against her bonds as she howled out loud.

Hisss!

Whack!

Almost without a pause the second stroke whipped in,

searing her right breast with six equally stinging tracks, spasms of pain lancing through her as she hung helpless and offered.

Hisss!
Whack!
Hisss!
Thwack!

The soft underside of each captive breast shook under the relentless onslaught, a dozen rapidly reddening weals marking out the path of the thongs as Marsha whipped in the lash with savage precision, each stroke sending a fresh tremor racing through Julia's spread-eagled limbs and drawing ever more shrill cries of anguish from her lips.

Four strokes only and already her breasts felt on fire. Tears sprang from her eyes, trickling freely down her cheeks and blurring her view of Marsha who stood back watching as Julia shuddered with each fresh spasm, unable to writhe or squirm so tightly was she bound to the bars.

"Two more."

Julia was sure she could take no more but secured as she was there was no choice and she watched helplessly as Marsha raised her arm again.

Hisss!
Thwack!
Hisss!
Crack!

The knotted thongs lashed down full across the taut swell of her breasts, searing the jutting buds of her nipples and imprinting her pale flesh with a cruel pattern of stinging stripes, each stripe a separate, burning line of pain that raced through her whole body. Her shrieks dissolved into low shuddering moans, her breasts heaving and glistening now with a sheen of perspiration.

Blinking back the tears that threatened to blind her she squinted down once more, seeing her captive and punished flesh reddening angrily, the redness underlaid with darker stripes where the lash had left its mark across her pale skin.

Marsha reached out to touch her, and she moaned again at the coolness of the fingers against the heat of the thrashing. Her moans deepened as Marsha found her still hard and throbbing nipples and caressed them gently.

A new and not unfamiliar sensation was replacing the raw stinging left by the lash, a feeling of wetness and warmth spreading slowly up from her belly, and she knew that despite the awfulness of her ordeal she was becoming aroused.

Marsha sensed it too and withdrew her fingers from Julia's now fully erect and tingling nipples.

"Not yet, Julia. Not just yet."

Wide eyed, her breathing shallow and ragged, Julia watched as Marsha reached into the pocket of her skirt and brought out a pair of small metal rings with small tabs attached so that they could be held up between forefinger and thumb.

Marsha held one up now to demonstrate how the ring was split at the top and opened out against a spring when the tabs were squeezed together.

Julia recognised the hated nipple rings at once, her stomach lurching at the thought of them being fitted to her still stinging breasts.

She wanted to beg for relief from yet more cruel restraint, however much she knew her pleas would fall on deaf ears, but the words wouldn't come.

"Such a wonderful discovery by Natalie, don't you think?"

Marsha had read the concern on her face and prolonged the suspense, snapping the rings open and closed as she moved nearer to her helpless victim.

Julia involuntarily tried to cringe away but could only watch helplessly as Marsha reached out for her once more, gripping one hard, swollen nipple firmly between her fingers pulling it out from her breast before attaching the first clip.

The metal was cold and tight around her already stinging flesh, bringing a gasp of pain to her lips. Then Marsha was gripping her other nipple and again the metal ring clamped shut on her tender buds. The throbbing pain drew a low sobbing moan from her.

"There now, that's just a little something to keep you alert. I'll see you in about an hour and arrange some exercises, but for now, as whipping you has made me so incredibly randy, I intend to get my lover to give me a good fucking.

A smile played about the corners of her mouth as she watched Julia's reaction, seeing the longing for freedom that could not be disguised.

"I'm sure that by the time I come back you'll be feeling randy too, so maybe if I'm pleased with you I'll get him to give you a good fucking while I watch."

She laughed lightly at the thought and turned away. Julia watched her go, breathing slowly and carefully against the throbbing ache already building in her breasts and closing her mind to the thoughts of what lay ahead.

Chapter Seventeen

It was a sore and weary Julia who returned to her apartment after two whole days at Marsha's country retreat. Each day she had been made to exercise for what seemed like hours on end until she had feared she would faint from sheer exhaustion.

Even worse than the constant exercise had been Marsha's insistence on demonstrating her own levels of fitness by carrying out the routines alongside her and meting out instant punishments whenever she considered Julia to be giving less than her best.

She carried the short, many thonged whip with her for that express purpose, lashing out at Julia without warning at any sign that she might be flagging.

That was disturbingly and painfully often, for although she tried her best she had constantly struggled to keep pace with the woman.

Julia learned that Marsha's ancestors had owned cotton plantations in America's deep south and it was not hard to imagine her harshly overseeing slave workers in those far off days.

In fact, Julia had rapidly come to the conclusion that Marsha regretted the passing of those times and was intent instead on relieving her frustrations by hard exercise.

Certainly, the limits to which Marsha seemed bent on pushing her bordered on the sadistic, as did the degree of punishment she was made to endure for failing to come up to standard. As she had promised, Marsha took every opportunity to whip her breasts, and to Julia's everlasting shame she had proved Marsha right by meekly offering up her breasts to the whip by the end of the very first day.

True, resistance would have been futile and carried the risk of greater punishment, but she still loathed her ready submission to something she hated so much.

Perversely, the whippings, while initially painful, had also been deeply arousing. Her nipples would persist in swelling and throbbing as she writhed and squirmed under the relentless bite of the slender thongs across her tender flesh.

The soft skin of her inner thighs and belly had also received much attention from Marsha's whip. The oil which had been rubbed so liberally into her skin had meant she was not so obviously marked, but she was still very sore and tender.

In between times she had pleasured Marsha, and again as Marsha had promised, Marsha's lover.

He watched her constantly, his state of arousal as he watched her exercise naked and then receive her punishments very obvious indeed. Whenever Marsha was finished with her she was turned over to him while Marsha herself showered and rested.

Marsha pointed out that she had actually met him before. He was one of the men she had pleasured at the Regency Hotel, the one who had made her suck him with no regard for her comfort or feelings.

He was no different now, interested only in his own pleasure, and while he fucked her several times, he was so quick with her that she did not reach orgasm once.

She could only conclude that he behaved very differently with Marsha, for she seemed well satisfied with him. Then it had struck her that after fucking her he invariably fucked Marsha not half an hour later.

She couldn't believe how stupid and naive she had been not to realise that by fucking her first he was able to prolong his next erection along with both his and Marsha's pleasure. The realisation stunned her.

She was being used merely as an aid to masturbation, a means of prolonging the pleasure of others without any regard at all for her feelings.

Never before had she felt so cheap and used. It was with a feeling of profound relief that she heard it was time for Marsha to return to her office and she to her apartment. Now, two days later, she was still upset about the episode and very confused about her feelings in general.

The time she had spent at the hunting lodge in the company of Bob and Mike, followed so closely by the cruel treatment she had received at the hands of Marsha and her lover seemed to bode ill for her immediate future.

She had harboured few illusions when she first began working for Nico, but to be used so casually was not what she wanted. None of her previous 'lovers' had used her in so callous a manner but now it seemed that things were changing.

From the little she knew of politics, she guessed that the current administration would be in office for at least four years and she wasn't sure she could take four years of submission to such self centred people.

On the other hand, keeping them sweet seemed to be important to the continued smooth running of Nico's operations, and that was of direct concern to her too.

Not for the first time, she found herself considering possible alternatives to what life was currently offering. She had enough money to return to England and support herself while she sorted out her life but she wasn't sure what she wanted to do.

The notion of a boyfriend and marriage flitted through her mind and she shook her head.

Her needs were different from those of other girls. Why that was so she wasn't sure, but she knew it to be true. She was born to be beaten! But surely she didn't need to be humiliated and abused every time she had sex in order to reach orgasm?

Then the idea hit her. Ricky! She could call Ricky, the manager of the gym where Marsha had taken her for that first gruelling session. His genuine desire for her had been very obvious. She had wanted him too! She had made no attempt to fight off the rape and her orgasm had been very satisfying.

She still had the address of the gym and she remembered that it closed for a few hours during the afternoon.

Her hand hovered over the telephone as she debated whether or not to call and suggest that they meet.

No. That would make her sound too eager and she still wasn't sure if she wanted to see Ricky again.

Still, there was a constant nagging inside of her and she took a deep breath as she came to her decision.

She would go to the gym and wait outside.

If Ricky came out and recognised her she would let fate take its course.

She felt suddenly breathless and excited as though she was back at school and about to break the rules or play truant and hurried down to the street before the feeling left her.

As though she had been given a sign, there was an empty cab cruising by. She settled herself comfortably in the back, paying no attention to the car pulling up behind.

There were two men in the car and they talked briefly, the driver glancing down at a photograph and nodding before pulling out to follow the cab at a discreet distance.

As on her earlier visit, the cab driver raised a questioning eyebrow at the address she gave him before deciding that it was none of his business and Julia settled back to collect her thoughts.

Now that she was on her way the whole idea seemed a

little foolish but she was too stubborn to go home.

In any case she felt she needed to prove something to herself even if it was just that she still retained some degree of independence.

The streets outside were becoming shabbier and she felt a knot of tension in her belly as the cab finally pulled up at the end of the block.

"There you go, lady, are you sure this is the right place?"

"Quite sure, thank you."

Julia peered around the run down neighbourhood as she paid off the cab, wondering if she should ask him to stay for a few minutes, then stiffened her shoulders, confident that she would be alright.

The gym was only a short way down the street, the door still open, and she began to walk slowly towards it.

Her heart was pounding and her legs felt suddenly weak.

The cab was turning around and she knew there was still time to call it back and forget the whole crazy idea - and then Ricky stepped into the street.

He was looking the other way at first and then as he locked the door he turned in her direction and his jaw dropped.

"Julia!"

"Just passing through..."

Her voice trailed away as she realised how stupid her explanation sounded, but Ricky didn't care.

"You come down here to work-out?"

She grinned, seeing him smile too at the memory.

"No chance, but you can maybe buy me a drink."

"Sure thing. There's a bar just down the street."

She nodded, relieved that it seemed to be so easy, and fell into step beside him as a thought occurred to her.

"I hope I won't be upsetting any girlfriends, Ricky."

"No, there's nobody special at the moment."

They reached the bar and he held the door open for her,

aware of the glances she was already attracting.

Julia was aware of them too.

They were glances that mentally undressed her and signalled envy at Ricky's good fortune and she was suddenly pleased that he seemed so well known around the neighbourhood.

Neither of them saw or took any notice of the car pulling up at the sidewalk opposite in violation of the no parking signs, as the two men inside settled themselves down to watch the door of the bar as it closed behind her.

The bar itself was just that and nothing more, a simply furnished room with four or five booths along one wall and a long, polished counter.

A few hardy afternoon drinkers glanced around as they entered, their glances lingering on Julia. She was pleased when Ricky steered her towards one of the booths.

"I guess this isn't the kind of place you're used to?"

His grin was half embarrassed half apologetic as she glanced around the room and smiled to reassure him.

"Don't worry about it, although I suppose a cocktail would be asking too much?"

"Well..."

"I'll settle for a cold beer."

Ricky looked relieved and called out the order as they arranged themselves on opposite sides of the narrow table.

"I guess I should have taken you somewhere better than this but you really took me by surprise turning up like that."

"I told you, don't worry about it."

Julia was wearing a light loose fitting dress that revealed a good portion of her breasts when she bent forward, and as she leaned across the table towards him she could see his eyes drawn irresistibly down.

"Anyway, you seem pleased to see me."

"Yes..."

"Me and my breasts?"

"Oh, well, yes..."

She continued leaning forward, displaying far more bravado than she actually felt.

"Why? You've seen them before."

Ricky's face reddened and she sat back as the barman arrived with the beer.

"That's in the past, Ricky. Forget it."

"It's kind of hard to forget. What was that all about anyway?"

"It concerns the people I work for and believe me, Ricky you don't need to know any more than that."

"Right. Fine."

He took a long drink from his glass and sat back looking at her thoughtfully.

Outside, a passing patrolman approached the car still parked under the no parking sign. The car window slid down, a few words were exchanged and a folded hundred dollar bill slipped unobtrusively into the patrolman's pocket. The car stayed where it was.

Back inside, Ricky was still struggling with his feelings and despite her nervousness Julia could feel herself becoming impatient.

After all, she hadn't sought him out just to sit drinking beer all afternoon and she was worried that her own new found confidence could suddenly evaporate.

"That last time, when I... you know?"

Julia leaned towards him again, noting how his eyes darted instinctively to her half revealed breasts.

"You mean when you took advantage and fucked me?"

"Well, yeah."

He was crimson with embarrassment, shifting uneasily in his seat.

"Like I said before, don't worry about it."

Julia took a deep breath and leaned further forward, lowering her voice to a husky whisper.

"Do you want to fuck me again, Ricky?"

"Of course I do!"

"Then why not come right out and say so?"

He coloured an even deeper shade of red.

"Well... you might say no."

"You haven't asked me yet."

There was a teasing smile on her lips as she watched his confusion.

"Hell, I'm not very good at this."

He took a deep breath and looked her full in the eye.

"OK, I fancy you like crazy, Julia, and I want to go to bed with you, right now."

"There, that didn't hurt at all."

Julia smiled and drained her glass.

"Do you live near here?"

"Yeah, two blocks down the street."

Ricky looked stunned at her ready acceptance, barely pausing to finish his own beer as he scrambled to his feet. Several drinkers exchanged knowing looks and eyed Julia up as she walked to the door but she ignored them.

She was committed now and she felt a heady rush of excitement and nervousness setting her legs trembling as she stepped back into the street.

"This way."

Ricky sounded nervous too, as though not sure that she wouldn't change her mind and leave him looking foolish. There was no chance of that.

She was determined now, light headed with a sudden sense of freedom that she hadn't felt in months as they hurried along the street to Ricky's apartment.

Like the rest of the neighbourhood, the building was neglected, paint peeling from the woodwork and garbage spilling onto the sidewalk outside, but she hardly noticed. Neither did she notice the car that had waited for them outside the bar cruising slowly down the street behind them and slotting into a space convenient for watching the apartment block.

Again the two men inside talked for a while before settling down to wait.

Chapter Eighteen

Julia hadn't expected much from Ricky's apartment and she was not disappointed. The place consisted of a small bed sitting room with a small kitchen and bathroom off and she was sure the walls were paper thin. She shrugged resignedly as she surveyed the narrow bed, reflecting that at least she had been fucked in worse places and it had been her choice to come here rather than book into a hotel. Ricky was both eager for her and apologetic about the run down state of the room but she shrugged again, her smile indicating that it really didn't matter.

"I didn't come here to admire the furnishings, Ricky."

With a deft movement she grasped the hem of her dress and pulled it over her head in one smooth movement, tossing it across the back of a nearby chair.

Her panties were next, peeled off and thrown on top of the dress.

She was naked now.

There was the familiar tingle in her belly that she always experienced when she was naked in the presence of a fully clothed man, and already her nipples were swelling. The bed was waiting and without preamble she lay down on it, rolling onto her back, one leg bent to reveal the merest hint of her sex.

"You're a little overdressed, Ricky."

Her voice was low and inviting and she watched through half closed eyes as he hurriedly tore off his clothes. He was already erect, his cock springing stiffly up in front of him as he walked towards her and she licked her lips at the thought of him thrusting it into her. His expression was both eager and bewildered as though he couldn't quite bring himself to believe that she had walked back into his life and calmly asked him to fuck her.

"You want me, don't you, Ricky?"

He nodded, his eyes lingering on the soft curves of her body. Her breasts were firm, jutting up towards him, the nipples dark and hard. He watched her breathlessly, his desire for her growing but wanting to prolong the pleasure of just looking at her as she lay waiting for him. For a few moments more he waited, his gaze moving down her body stretched out so openly on the narrow bed, taking in the flat plane of her stomach, the long, smooth lines of her thighs and, nestling in between, the rounded swell of her pubis, prominent and inviting.

He wanted her badly now, had wanted her since the moment she had left the gym after that first punishing workout. Punishing in every sense of the word he reminded himself, conjuring up a mental picture of her writhing and squirming helplessly as the woman, Marsha, had whipped her. He had cringed a little himself as the strap cracked down savagely across her tender flesh but had been unable to tear his eyes away from the erotic spectacle.

The whipping had aroused her, excited her in some strange way and he had reaped the benefit.

His cock twitched at the memory and he wondered briefly if she would allow him to whip her too. He shook his head, almost laughing at the thought. She was here, in his apartment, lying naked on his bed and he was going to fuck her. That was enough for now. Unable to restrain his desire for her any longer, Ricky slipped onto the bed alongside her and reached out to caress her breasts.

She stirred at his touch but watched him through half closed eyes as he withdrew his hand for a few moments before returning to trail his fingers around the tight buds of her nipples.

Julia murmured softly, moving her body ever so slightly as though dragging herself from a deep sleep as all the while his fingers stroked and teased her swelling nipples until they jutted out from her breasts in hard quivering arousal and between her thighs a warm dampness began to spread.

Her lower belly was beginning to throb like a second pulse, speeding up and enfolding her whole body until she could not hold back her own all consuming desire. She moaned softly and arched her back, hands reaching down to grasp and fondle Ricky's by now fully engorged cock.

Ricky gasped aloud with pleasure at her touch, reaching out for her, pulling the length of her body fully against his own and rolling over onto his back so she lay astride him, the moistly parted lips of her sex pressing down on his throbbing shaft.

Squirming now with pleasure, she bent forwards, rubbing her breasts across his chest as she felt his hands slipping down her flanks to mould around and grasp the taut, smooth swelling of her buttocks.

For a few moments he held her still. Then he pulled upwards, sliding her up his body, his cock escaping from the soft press of her belly to push up insistently between her open thighs, brushing against the now hot and swollen inner lips of her sex, sliding easily over the warm wetness of her arousal.

Pressing her hands down on the bed she arched her back tight, offering up her breasts and nipples to Ricky's eager tongue while she bore down hard against his grip on her bottom, feeling for him with those pulsing lips, wanting him inside her, hard and thrusting.

She pushed back hard, found him, smeared him with her juices, pushed harder, her breath rasping harshly as Ricky's tongue flicked rapidly across her jutting breasts, then his lips closed firmly around the hard swell of one aching nipple, sucking so hard that she shuddered in a turmoil of passion and frustration. He gripped her tighter, pulling the cheeks of her buttocks apart, easing her back up his body and away from the engorged cock that she craved, prolonging his own pleasure and deepening her desire for him.

Again she bore down and again Ricky relaxed his grip ever so slightly and again she found him, enfolding him in the now dripping lips of her vagina, feeling him slipping against, the trembling pit of her belly, then up into it.

He stretched her wide and she leaned forward, bracing her hands on his chest, thrusting down onto his thickness. Her breasts pulled away from his mouth and dangled like ripe fruit above his face, swaying erotically as she began to wriggle her hips from side to side, settling herself firmly astride his throbbing shaft.

He darted out his tongue, teasing her nipples before sucking one swollen bud back between his lips, and she moaned gently in response.

"Fuck me, Ricky! Fuck me hard!"

He smiled at the lewd invitation and jerked his hips clear of the bed, burying himself deeper inside her.

His hands gripped her hips, holding her steady and rolling her onto her back once more.

She lay sprawled diagonally across the narrow bed, legs dangling to one side and her shoulders hanging clear of the other.

Her back was arched, her breasts and belly thrusting up. Ricky lay between her spread thighs, the full length of his cock jammed deep into her sex.

Slowly he began to thrust in and out of her and she arched her back higher to meet each thrust, dragging him deep into her, her belly grinding against his.

"Come on... fuck me... fuck me..."

He responded again, grasping her buttocks and reaming her oozing slit, his cock making soft sucking noises as it slipped easily in and out of her.

"Harder... fuck me harder!"

She could feel her passion rising but there was no urgency in the spasms of pleasure rippling through her body.

Something was missing and she knew Ricky would climax first and leave her frustrated and unfulfilled.

Her body was alive with arousal but she remained teetering on the brink of orgasm.

Ricky was thrusting hard and steadily into her and she was responding to his every thrust but still her passions remained locked up inside her.

"Harder... harder... harder."

She was almost screaming at him, her belly smacking against his in a desperate attempt to drive herself towards a climax. Ricky was going to come first, she could feel it, feel the urgent throbbing and swelling of his cock buried so deep inside her.

Her heart was pounding, sweat beading her body as she writhed beneath him... then there was a pounding at the door of the apartment and Ricky jerked out of her.

He climaxed as he did so, hot jets of sperm splashing wet and sticky onto her belly and breasts while she wailed in confusion.

Then the flimsy door crashed open.

Cursing, Ricky rolled from the bed, toppling Julia onto the floor. She sprawled awkwardly, gasping and quivering, her elusive orgasm slipping further and further from her as she took in what was happening around her.

Two men burst into the room, their actions confident and assured, their eyes taking in every detail.

Ricky lunged at one of them but the man sidestepped easily, sticking out a foot to send him sprawling to the floor.

"Take it easy. We've come for her."

He jerked a thumb in Julia's direction, his eyes glinting as they lingered on her nakedness.

"Time to go, Julia, the boss man wants to see you."

Julia was confused, embarrassed too by his lecherous stare.

"But... he's out of town."

"Yeah. He sent us to fetch you."

There was something wrong about the set up.

She had never seen these two before and yet they knew her and had obviously managed to track her down to Ricky's apartment. She felt a stab of panic at the thought that Nico had somehow found out about her little show of independence and disapproved of it.

On the floor, Ricky started to get up but one of the men motioned him to stay where he was.

"This has nothing to do with you, so just stay cool and keep your mouth shut."

"Julia? Who the hell are these guys?"

He was bewildered and she suddenly feared he would do something stupid and get hurt.

"It, it's alright, Ricky. I have to go now, that's all."

He was still confused and she looked at the two men.

"You won't hurt him, will you?"

"So long as he's a good boy."

She breathed a small sigh of relief and climbed from the bed, heading for the small bathroom.

"Where are you going?"

"To get cleaned up..."

She gestured vaguely at her sperm spattered body, blushing again as the man leered at her.

"If you need a cloth, use this."

Scooping up her discarded panties he tossed them at her and now she was certain that something was wrong.

Nico's men might leer at her if they caught sight of her naked, but otherwise they treated her politely, unlike these two.

To add to her disquiet, his companion had shut the door of the apartment and was leaning against it.

She began to wipe herself clean and then a question occurred to her and she jerked her head up.

"Why couldn't you wait until I left or at least knock on the door like normal people instead of just bursting in on us like that?"

"More fun this way! At least we gave him a chance to slip his dick into you."

Both of them grinned at her and she felt her disquiet deepen as the man licked his lips, his eyes narrowing.

"Is she a good lay? She sure sounded good!"

Julia dropped the now sticky panties and reached for her dress, uneasy at the way the conversation was progressing. Presumably these two were recent employees and had confused her with some cheap whore and she was sure they intended to overstep the mark.

Their next words confirmed her fears and her heart sank.

"I could go for a piece of her myself."

Julia froze, glancing quickly up at the one who had spoken. He was staring insolently at her, his fingers already busy at his belt.

His companion too was staring at her as he nodded agreement.

"Yeah. No hurry, eh?"

Julia shrank back, her heart beginning to pound madly as she contemplated her predicament.

"I don't think that's a good idea, guys."

"Oh?"

She took a deep breath and faced him, her eyes flashing.

"You know who I am?"

"Sure, so what?"

"I'll tell Nico!"

"I'll take my chance."

He shrugged again, grinning broadly as he slid his zipper down and now Julia really was gripped by panic.

They intended to fuck her right here and now and neither one of them cared about the possible consequences.

Ricky sensed her confusion, wriggling round to face her.

"What's wrong, Julia?"

"Nothing."

"That's right, son, just like the lady says, now be quiet and we'll let you watch."

Both men laughed out loud and Julia shuddered. She was suddenly convinced that these men did not work for Nico. They were about to rape her and Ricky looking on would spur them to show off and fuck her as hard as they could.

Her earlier panic was subsiding, replaced by the familiar feeling of helpless resignation.

She was going to be fucked whether she wanted it or not and there was nothing she could do about it except submit and get the whole unpleasant business over with as soon as possible.

Her heart was still pounding but otherwise she felt almost calm and detached as she watched both men strip. They were already excited, cocks jutting fat and heavy from their bellies. She swallowed in dread at the thought of them penetrating her.

"Come here!"

The man nearest to her beckoned and she walked slowly across the room, determined not to betray the apprehension she felt. Her bare breasts swayed gently as she moved and she could see him looking at them, his eyes shining with anticipation. Ricky was looking up at her too, his own anxieties forgotten as he took in the sight of her nakedness.

The man grabbed her and spun her around to face his

companion, his cock thrusting urgently against her back. His hands cupped and lifted her breasts for inspection, fondling her roughly.

"Tits look good to me!"

"They feel good too."

The man chuckled, squeezing her firm flesh until she gasped and then it happened.

Without warning a surge of arousal flooded her and without looking down she knew that her nipples were swelling and hardening without even being touched.

She wanted to laugh out loud at the craziness of it all. She had given herself willingly to Ricky and her orgasm had eluded her. Now, standing naked and helpless between the two men who would soon be fucking her only for their own pleasure, she was aroused and filled with lust. Her condition did not go unnoticed by Joe.

"Hellfire, Wes, you sure got her worked up in a hurry, look at her tits."

Wes didn't bother looking, merely slipping his hands further up the taut swell of her breasts until he could feel her nipples pressing against his palms.

He rubbed her breasts in a hard, circular motion, stimulating her further until she wriggled involuntarily against him, a low moan escaping from her lips.

Joe reached for her too, his hand delving between her thighs. She moaned again, knowing what he would find. Sure enough, his hand came away glistening with her ever increasing arousal. His eyes widened in appreciation.

"Gee, Wes, I never felt a girl so wet before... she must want it real bad."

Wes squeezed her breasts again, his face pressing close up alongside hers, peering down at her body.

"Is that right? Do you want to be fucked?"

She squirmed in his grasp, sharp spasms of pleasure racking her body as Joe delved between her thighs once more.

"Yes... yes, damn you!"

Joe was gripping the swelling inner lips of her sex between his fingers, squeezing and pulling at the wet, pliant folds of flesh as though milking her. In a way he was, for she could feel her wetness seeping steadily out onto her thighs, bathing his fingers as he fondled her so lewdly.

Unable to restrain herself she moaned out loud, jerking her hips forward, breasts heaving.

"Ahhhhh... please... please..."

Wes gave her breasts another squeeze and spun her around, pushing her towards the narrow bed.

"Up, kneel up with your legs open."

She knew what he wanted and scrambled onto the bed, kneeling on all fours with her legs spread wide.

Behind her she heard the coarse comments and laughter and she flushed hotly, wishing Ricky wasn't present to witness her humiliating and shameless submission.

"You! Get over in the corner where I can keep an eye on you."

Ricky shuffled shamefaced into the corner and then Joe called him back, whispering excitedly to Wes.

Julia tensed, fearing they were about to harm him in some way but even she was totally unprepared for what they had in mind.

"Looks like you've got a hard on there, son."

"Yes..."

Ricky's voice was barely a whisper.

"Seems like a shame to waste it so why not kneel up in front of the girl here and she can suck you off while we fuck her."

"No! No way am I getting involved in this."

Julia tensed again. The suggestion had stunned her too but unlike Ricky she knew there wasn't any question of choice.

"Do it Ricky."

"But..."

"Please, Ricky!"

There was a long moment of silence and then Ricky climbed up and knelt in front of her, his almost fully erect cock swaying beneath her face. A thin smear of sperm still glistened on the tip and she could smell the heavy musk of her earlier arousal. She glanced up at him, a weak smile of encouragement on her lips.

"Don't worry, it'll be all right."

"Sure it will, sister. Now, start sucking."

Wes slapped her across her upthrust backside, the smack sounding loud in the room and she bent quickly forward to take Ricky between her lips. At least they weren't going to whip her, for which she felt a surge of relief.

Presumably whoever had sent them for her, and she was now convinced it wasn't Nico, had told them to deliver her unmarked.

She could sense them both close up behind her and another shudder rippled through her as she felt one of them kneel up on the bed between her legs. Her thighs were spread very wide and her sex gaped openly, wet and inviting. Between her lips she could feel Ricky swelling and hardening still further as she sucked him deeper into her mouth, and a tremor of arousal stirred in her as she imagined the lewd display she was presenting.

This time when she was penetrated she knew she would climax and she wriggled her hips in anticipation.

"Hey, kid, don't just sit there, play with her tits or something."

"Yeah, she might as well enjoy herself too."

Both Wes and Joe laughed out loud at the crude suggestion but Ricky hesitated, his hands hovering above his knees.

"Mmmmmph!"

With her mouth stuffed full of his rapidly swelling cock, Julia could only wriggle her hips and grunt in encouragement, anxious not to annoy the two men behind her.

"See, she wants it."

"Yeah, just grab hold and hang on tight while we give her a ride she won't forget."

More coarse laughter rang out and then Ricky's hands closed around her breasts, her nipples pressed hard down into his palms. Hands grasped her flanks, lifting her a little, and she felt the first brush of a cock between the dripping lips of her sex.

Whether it was Joe or Wes she neither knew nor cared. Her whole body was alive with arousal and trembling with the need for release. Her hips wriggled again as she pushed back, urging the thick shaft of flesh further into her belly, bathing it with her freely flowing juices. Her hips rose and her breasts pressed even harder against Ricky's now gently fondling hands sending a tremor rippling through her. Wes leered at her ready submission and lunged deep into her, filling her and stretching her wide. She pitched forward, her gasp of pleasure choked off by the hardness of Ricky's cock spearing deeper into her mouth.

"Suck him hard..."

Julia needed no urging. The feel of the cock buried deep in her sex triggered a familiar feeling of madness inside her and she pushed back hard against him, thrusting her backside up as she plunged her mouth down on Ricky. Her breasts swung wildly as Wes pumped his cock in and out of her, his belly smacking loudly into her backside with each stroke, driving her forward onto the cock clamped between her lips.

He was excited, pumping her faster and faster as his climax approached, but Julia knew she would come first. She was hot already, gasping for breath as her belly shuddered and heaved and her orgasm broke in long sweeping waves.

Wes slammed into her one last time, stiffening against her as his cock swelled and jetted a stream of sperm deep into her while she bucked and heaved beneath him. Her cries were muffled by Ricky's cock. Then he was coming too, driven to a climax by the relentless stimulation of her lips and tongue and the sight of her being fucked. His hands gripped her hard as his sperm spattered her throat and filled her mouth and she swallowed greedily, choking and gagging and gasping for breath as her own orgasm subsided.

Wes slipped out of her, his place taken at once by Joe and she steadied herself for his first thrust. His cock slipped easily into her sex and withdrew at once, glistening with a sheen of her juices.

"Damn it, Wes, you left her wide open."

"Then stick it in her ass."

Julia tensed and forced herself to relax as Joe gripped her buttocks, prising her still wider. She was used to being penetrated there but the first few thrusts as she was opened up wide could still hurt.

She clenched her teeth.

Joe's cock slid wetly along the crease of her backside, pressing urgently at the tight puckered opening. Face now buried in Ricky's lap, Julia pushed back, breathing deeply and matching him thrust for thrust until with a soft sucking sound he slipped into her.

The pain came at once, a sharp stabbing as he forced her wider and slid irresistibly deeper inside her. She twisted and heaved, breath now coming in short panting gasps, and then he was filling her and the pain was replaced by a welcoming rush of pleasure.

She was stuffed full of hot throbbing cock, the sensitive and tender membranes of her vagina squeezed in on themselves, and rubbing together as the man buggered her relentlessly. Between her legs her sex bulged out, quivering and pulsating with a seeming life of its own. Her body was hot and dripping with sweat. She moaned and gasped with each renewed thrust, squirming desperately around the shaft of flesh impaling her. She could feel every throbbing inch of it as it reamed her, the tremors pulsing within her growing stronger and more urgent with every lunge.

Higher and higher she thrust her backside, her breasts pressing down onto the bed, nipples tingling as they brushed back and forth over the rough sheet. Spasms of pain overlaid with pleasure stabbed through her, the pleasure becoming more and more intense until the first rush of her orgasm overwhelmed her. Her belly spasmed, gripping Joe's cock hard, squeezing the rigid shaft tight and triggering his climax.

His rhythm faltered, his hips jerking spasmodically as he pumped his load of hot sticky cream into her. Julia could feel it, could feel the twitching and spurting deep inside her, and then her own orgasm swept over her in an uncontrolled flood and she collapsed forward into Ricky's lap, writhing and crying out aloud in the sheer joy of release.

"Man! That was some wild ride!"

Joe slipped out of her and knelt behind her, wide eyed, his chest heaving as he witnessed the last throes of her explosive orgasm. Julia didn't hear him. She lay trembling and exhausted, her body still hot and glistening with perspiration, sticky sperm oozing from her.

She had been used and abused and she had revelled unashamedly in the experience. She wondered briefly what the men watching must think of her and was surprised to discover that she didn't really care.

Wes prodded her in the ribs and she rolled over without shame to face him.

"You look a mess, girl. Go clean yourself up."

She half walked, half staggered to the bathroom and showered thoroughly, washing every trace of sperm from her body while Wes watched her from the door.

"Here, I suppose you'd better put this on."

He tossed her dress to her and she breathed a small sigh of relief that she wasn't going to be taken naked from the apartment.

"What about Ricky?

"Joe's had a word with the kid and he knows to keep his mouth shut."

"You didn't hurt him?"

"Course not, he's a sensible kid and doesn't need things spelling out."

Julia breathed another sigh of relief. Whatever trouble lay ahead for her she was sure she could cope with it - and at least she hadn't dragged Ricky down with her. Her panties lay in a wet, sticky heap by the side of the bed.

"You need these?"

Wes kicked them towards her, his expression sneering. She wondered if he would order her to put them on anyway.

"I guess not."

She slipped the dress over her head and faced Wes squarely, her expression giving no hint of the turmoil inside.

"Let's go."

Chapter Nineteen

If Julia still held any doubts that Wes and Joe worked for Nico, they were dispelled the moment she saw their car. Unlike the stretch limousines favoured by Nico and Natalie, this was just a normal family saloon. Wes drove and Joe climbed into the back with Julia. There could be little chance of escape as both the door handles and window winders had been removed.

"Where are we going?"

"You'll find out soon enough."

They left the city, turning off the main highway onto a number of secondary roads. Julia was soon hopelessly confused. There was little chance of recognising a landmark in case she could escape.

After about half an hour the car turned down what was obviously a private road and through gaps in the trees she caught glimpses of a substantial looking house on a hill top.

A few moments later the car drew up outside an imposing gateway, the road continuing in zig zags up the steep hillside. As Julia peered through the car windows, expecting some kind of welcoming committee, Wes left his seat and opened the rear doors, indicating with a brusque jerk of his thumb that she was to join him outside.

"From here, you walk."

Again he jerked his thumb, this time pointing out the road which wound its way up the side of the hill to the house at the top, its surface shimmering in the late afternoon heat. She looked longingly back into the shaded interior of the car before an impatient snap of the man's fingers set her moving slowly forwards.

There was little shade and almost at once perspiration beaded her body as she walked, soaking through the thin fabric of her dress.

Behind her the car began moving once more, keeping station a few feet behind her as though to urge her on. She envied the driver his air conditioned comfort as she brushed a hand across her heated brow. The long skirt which she had earlier welcomed so eagerly now clung to her legs, impeding her progress as she toiled upwards. The slope was much steeper than it had first seemed and she was suddenly glad of the fitness exercises she had been so rigorously put through.

By the time she reached the broad tree-shaded patio in front of the house every muscle in her legs was aching, and if it were not for the persistent presence of the car so close behind her and the fact that she was sure she was being observed from the house itself, she would have been forced to stop and rest.

The car pulled up alongside her now, both men indicating a narrow arch. She trudged through it wearily, tempted to linger in the cool shade but certain that someone on the other side would be expecting her.

At first she thought she was mistaken, for the courtyard into which she emerged appeared empty. Then she caught sight of a young girl watching her from the shade of a deep set doorway and she halted, uncertain of what was now required of her.

For what seemed like an age they stared silently at one another, Julia tired and dripping with perspiration from her long climb up the hill and the other girl cool and relaxed as she rested in the shade until at last she got to her feet and stepped out into the courtyard.

Now Julia could see that she was bringing with her a

large earthenware water jar, the sight reminding her of how thirsty she was and she licked her lips eagerly at the prospect of a drink. She had to drink from her cupped hands as the girl tipped the water from the jar. The water spilled down her chin and onto her dress as she greedily drank her fill, but she didn't mind, grateful for the chance to cool herself down, splashing yet more water over her face when she had finished.

The girl looked on silently, her expression mildly curious, and when the jar was finally empty she beckoned Julia to follow her, pointing out two crosses marked on the ground and only then did she break her silence.

"You must wait here until Mr Carlos is ready to see you."

Carlos! So it was Carlos who had sent the two men to abduct her. This was bad. Carlos had made no secret of his interest in her when they had first met at the bistro and as he now had her without Nico's permission she was sure he would want to make the risk he was running worthwhile.

"Stand on those marks."

Julia nodded, placing her feet exactly on the two marks and clasping her arms behind her in the now instinctive posture, glad that the marks were placed to allow her to stand in the shade of the wide verandah that ran all around the courtyard rather than out in the middle in the harsh glare of the sun. She had no idea how long Carlos would make her wait, although she guessed that he was probably observing her from some unseen vantage point.

She resisted the urge to stare about her and relaxed as much as her submissive pose would allow, and waited, full of dread.

Presently a door banged open and two servants entered the courtyard carrying a small table which they placed in the shade a few feet away from where Julia stood. Two more servants followed, one carrying a chair and the other bearing a tray holding a flask of wine and a glass. All four regarded her with the same open curiosity shown by the mysterious girl, smiling at her knowingly before retiring back into the house. She heard them laughing among themselves as she continued to wait. No doubt both Wes and Joe had boasted of their experiences with her and she fidgeted with sudden embarrassment.

Time passed slowly, the shadows in the courtyard lengthening. Then at last she heard the door open once more and watched from the corner of her eye as Carlos entered and stood looking at her quietly for a few moments.

"So! Mine at last, Julia."

Julia remained silent, staring straight ahead as Carlos settled himself in the chair. Wine gurgled from the flask as he poured himself a drink and it was all she could do to prevent herself shifting nervously under his steady scrutiny. She had a fair idea of just how much power Nico wielded and yet Carlos was sitting calmly, apparently not at all concerned at having kidnapped her.

"I feel I should apologise for the excess of zeal shown by my men, but looking at you I suppose they can hardly be blamed as you were apparently quite naked when they caught up with you."

Julia's cheeks flamed crimson and she bit her lip as she realised they would have spared no detail in telling their tale.

"Well they have an advantage over me so let me take a good look at you too... get rid of that dress."

Carlos waved his hand towards her, an expectant smile playing on his lips. There was no point in refusing. She was sure the house was full of servants who would willingly strip her naked on Carlos' orders. She took a deep breath to steady herself but she was aware that already her heart was beginning to beat a little faster. She reached down for the hem of her dress. Crossing her arms she grasped the hem and slowly raised the skirt up the length of her thighs.

Carlos watched her intently, leaning forward a little as she reached the top of her legs. She hesitated for a few seconds, postponing the moments before she revealed her nakedness beneath the dress. Then she lifted her arms, raising the skirt in one smooth movement. Carlos sucked in his breath at his first sight of her shaved sex, the lips puffy and plainly visible between her parted thighs.

"Looks to me like you get fucked a lot, Julia!"

Julia's face burned red at the crude remark, but Carlos was leaning forward, demanding an answer.

"Well? Do you?"

"I-I-I suppose so."

"You suppose so? What do you mean by that?"

Julia stood nervously, not raising her dress any higher as she struggled to frame a suitable reply to the deeply intimate questioning.

"Do you get fucked every day?"

"Not every day."

"But most days?"

Carlos persisted, clearly enjoying her embarrassment and confusion and Julia hesitated, realising that he was leading her into some kind of trap.

"It depends on what Nico wants."

She hoped that the mention of Nico would bring some kind of reaction, perhaps remind Carlos of the risk he was running but he carried on goading her.

"So if Nico tells you to fuck a guy every day then you'll do just that?"

"Yes."

"What if he tells you to fuck three or four guys at the same time, you'll do that too?"

Julia could now see where the questioning was leading and she fumbled for a reply.

"Yes."

"But what about your feelings, Julia? Would you really want to fuck three or four guys at the same time?"

Carlos leaned forward, baiting her as she struggled to avoid any more damaging admissions.

"What it comes down to in the end, Julia, is whether you're a slave or a fucking whore."

Julia flushed at how easily he had understood her confusion but Carlos wasn't about to let her off the hook.

"So which is it, Julia, slave or whore?"

She wished the ground would open up and swallow her but Carlos was still leaning forward, demanding an answer.

"I'm his slave."

"What was that? I guess I didn't hear so good."

"I said, I'm a slave."

Julia was sure that her shouted reply could be clearly heard by everyone inside the house, but suddenly it didn't seem to matter. Here she was, standing in full view of anyone watching from the windows, with her dress pulled up to her waist revealing her nakedness beneath - and becoming aroused too, despite her lewd display, her body reacting to the helplessness of her situation.

Carlos leaned further forward and she was sure he could see that her sex lips were more swollen and open than when she had first exposed them to his eager scrutiny.

"Belt you if you don't oblige, does he?"

She nodded.

"Well, I'm glad we got that sorted out at last. I wouldn't feel good about entertaining some cheap whore."

Julia bit her lip, waiting for him to goad her again, perhaps remarking on her very obviously growing state of arousal, but he settled back comfortably again and she relaxed. She was Nico's slave because she wanted to be: she could walk away any time but she did not because she gloried in it. Slave or tramp or whore, what did it matter?

"You going to take that dress off all the way or just

stand there advertising what you've got between your legs?"

Julia flinched at the casual insult and then her resolve took over and she hauled the dress over her head, tossing it aside in one smooth movement.

"Nice tits, good nipples too. I bet they get sucked an awful lot."

Julia nodded, not trusting herself to speak for fear of falling into another trap but he was more interested in just looking at her in quiet appreciation.

"Yes, real nice tits. I guess you'll be feeling my hands around them before much longer..."

Defiance flared through her and for a few moments. She spat on the ground, knowing that she would have to submit to him but wanting him to know that it was not by choice. Carlos chuckled and took a long drink.

"You've got spirit. I like that, but we both know you won't really put up much of a fight, don't we?"

Julia hesitated and Carlos took another sip of wine, enjoying her uncertainty.

"I've talked to guys who've had you and they all say the same. You behave all shocked and ladylike, but the moment you're stripped and maybe tied down or whipped a little, you come on real strong like there's no stopping you."

Julia knew he was right. The evidence was plain to see in her now open and inviting sex and the hard swelling of her nipples as she responded to the public exposure of her body for his amusement. For a few moments more he watched her intently and now, from the corner of her eye she could see the men who had brought out the table and chairs crowding into one side of the courtyard for a better view. Both Wes and Joe were there too, nudging each other and laughing.

Was she going to be gang banged by them all? Her stomach lurched at the thought. She was helpless to resist and that very fact sent a wave of lust rippling through her as she contemplated being used by the men in full view of the household, merely to entertain the man watching her so intently. It seemed as though Carlos could read her mind as he glanced across at the small crowd before returning his attention to her now obvious state of arousal. He grinned and motioned the men to move closer and stand alongside his chair.

"Well, as we've got you all worked up just by looking I suppose you'd better let us have a real good look at what you've got."

He swivelled one finger round and Julia understood at once, her face flaring deep red in embarrassment. Turning her back to her grinning audience, she spread her legs wide and bent to grasp her ankles. Her backside tightened, jutting out towards them, the now wet and open lips of her sex gaping wide, while between her parted thighs, her breasts were clearly visible as they dangled heavily down. Every inch of her body was now lewdly displayed and she stood as still as she could, ignoring the coarse comments passing among the watching men.

Footsteps sounded on the stones of the courtyard and she tensed, expecting to be touched, perhaps even penetrated by a probing finger.

"See, Carlos, I told you she was a pretty little thing."

Julia gave a start and despite herself, half turned towards the voice, unable to believe her ears.

Marsha! It was Marsha!

Her mind raced, unsure what Marsha was doing in the company of Carlos. Her stomach lurched again at the memory of how the woman had so recently used her.

"Stay as you are!"

Julia obeyed at once, although her legs were now shaking both from the strain of holding her shameful position and anxiety at being once more at the mercy of the sadistic Marsha. From her brief glance she had seen the many thonged whip dangling from Marsha's hand and she knew it would not be long before the thongs were lashing her most tender flesh.

"You have been having a fine time to yourself Julia, but with Ricky of all people."

Marsha's tone was mocking and Julia could feel herself flushing hot.

"What was the attraction, Julia?"

Julia said nothing, aware that to speak would only make the situation worse.

"Was it the work out he gave you, Julia? Did you fancy a repeat performance or was it something else?"

"The kid was giving her a lot more than a work out when we got there."

"Yeah, the randy little bitch was begging for it when we got there. We could hear her halfway down the hall."

Joe's comments triggered a wave of laughter among the watchers. It was so unfair. It was true that in many ways Ricky wasn't a partner she would normally have chosen, but they were making the whole episode sound cheap and tawdry. It was Wes and Joe who had behaved the worst and nobody was saying a word about their behaviour, blaming her instead as if she had led them on and encouraged them.

"Yes, she is something of a slut, after all, look at how brazenly she's standing here showing everything she's got."

Again Julia bit her lip, wanting to stand up defiantly and refute what was being said about her but knowing the futility of such an act.

"Girls like Julia... well I guess they deserve whatever they've got coming to them."

Marsha's tone was careless, dismissive and Julia shuddered at the thought of the whip trailing from her hand. The woman was standing alongside her now, dangling the lash just in front of her jutting backside. Julia could see it as she peered back between her legs. The sight fascinated her, drawing her eyes.

The watching men were silent, their eyes on the lash as Marsha casually swung her wrist back, allowing the thongs to smack smartly between Julia's spread thighs. The impact was not too hard but Julia's reaction was immediate. The lips of her sex quivered and pulsated against the slap of the leather.

Again the thongs swung out and back and again she responded, her sex opening wider as though to admit the thrusting cock of an unseen lover. She moaned in despair at her body's betrayal, feeling her juices spilling out to dampen the tender flesh of her inner thighs as Marsha continued to swing her wrist back and forth, again and again, moaning and squirming in despair at the spectacle she knew she was presenting.

She almost wished that Marsha would really swing back her arm and lash into her without mercy, painful though she knew that would be. To writhe helpless and howling under the lash seemed suddenly better than the long drawn out torment of the insistent gentle slap of the thongs against her distended sex lips, as each smack of the leather against her flesh opened her wider and dragged her one slow step nearer to orgasm.

The men were noisy again, coarse laughter and comment greeting every stroke of the whip. Her face was hot and red and her breasts throbbed and tingled as she squirmed and wriggled under the relentless stimulation, but orgasm eluded her. Marsha was careful, timing each swing of the whip to avoid tipping her over the edge, ensuring that she remained fully aroused, sex lips quivering and inviting, shudders racking her body until her moans turned into urgent pleas for release.

Her thighs glistened with the juices flowing from her and her breath rasped harshly in her throat. Satisfied, Marsha nodded to Carlos who staggered to his feet, transfixed by

Julia's slowly writhing body.

His erection bulged against his jeans and as he tugged down the zipper, his heavy cock sprang free, swaying and throbbing eagerly. Julia's eyes were squeezed shut and she didn't see the whip lifted clear as Carlos positioned himself behind her, half turning to grin broadly at his audience before plunging deep into her yearning sex.

She cried out loud at the shock of penetration as his belly smacked wetly into hers and then her orgasm seized her, ripping through her like a flood. Spasm after spasm racked her and she bucked and heaved with each thrust of his cock. He reached under her, searching for her breasts and she cried out louder as his fingers closed around her swollen and throbbing nipples, breasts swinging wildly as she struggled to keep her feet against the shudders surging through her.

The fact that she was giving such a shameless display of abandon in a public place mattered nothing as she revelled in the relief of her pent up passions. She didn't care that Carlos who was fucking her so enthusiastically and Marsha who was still standing close alongside her had manipulated her so easily. All that mattered was the sweet release of orgasm, the all consuming spasms racing through her again and again.

At last she sagged, spent and gasping, legs trembling, held up only by the firm grip Carlos had on her perspiration drenched breasts.

When he pulled out of her she staggered, almost falling to her knees before she could bring herself under control. She was becoming aware of her surroundings again, the excited babble of conversation behind her as the men crowded around Carlos. She wondered again if Carlos was going to let them all fuck her and realised that she didn't care.

Not even the threatening presence of Marsha troubled

her as she felt a hand on her bottom and heard the order to stand up straight and turn around. She faced them calmly, very aware that her breasts were still hard and swollen, her thighs glistening with streaks of sperm, the scent of sexual arousal and release heavy in the air around her.

She was tired and confused, her body still tingling with arousal and lust. Yet again she had experienced a shattering orgasm by being forced against her will. She shook her head in resignation and squared her shoulders, breasts jutting proudly as she faced them.

Carlos flicked his gaze over her, his eyes shining with approval.

"You may be just a little slut but you'll do me just fine, Julia, now get cleaned up and join Marsha and myself for dinner."

Julia saw everyone leaving and hesitated only briefly before following them towards the house. The men constantly glanced back at her, nudging one another and grinning openly and she felt glad when she passed into the house to be taken in charge by a maid who led her quickly away to the quarters that had been prepared for her.

Chapter Twenty

Dinner was served in a small dining room.

Julia sat naked at the table, flanked by Carlos and Marsha's lover.

The meal itself was a gourmet delight and all the more welcome to Julia as she had not eaten since breakfast. Carlos himself was a perfect host, encouraging her to eat and drink her fill although she was not allowed to forget her status. Marsha had insisted on fitting her with nipple rings before the meal and both men took full advantage of her nearness, constantly fondling her breasts and stroking the soft skin of her inner thighs until the nagging ache in her breasts was overlaid with a heated flush of arousal.

She fully expected to be fucked at some point by Carlos and Marsha's lover and yet she could accept that with a readiness that even now amazed her.

The meal over, all four retired to the study. Carlos sat behind the desk while two of his men busied themselves pouring brandy for everyone except Julia before taking up station by the door. Julia stood uncertainly in the middle of the room until Marsha beckoned her over to where she was sitting.

"Here, Julia, come and sit beside me."

She patted the arm of her chair and Julia perched unsteadily alongside her.

"That's right. I think its my turn to play with your tits, don't you?"

Julia shuddered as she felt the woman's fingers trailing across her breasts and lingering over her jutting nipples, feeling the heat of arousal surging through her belly once more until she could contain herself no longer and moaned aloud.

"Does that feel good?"

Julia could not deny her need. Her thighs were already damp with the juices glistening on the open and inviting lips of her sex.

"You want to come, don't you?"

"Yes, oh yes."

The admission sent a stab of shame through her but it was the truth.

"Then get down on your knees and beg."

"No! You don't own me and I won't beg!"

Marsha laughed at Julia's outburst and reached out once more to fondle her breast. Carlos was smiling broadly too, and Julia felt a sudden heaviness in the pit of her stomach, a wrenching certainty that all was not right.

"Shall we tell her, Carlos?"

Julia attempted to twist away from Marsha's persistent fondling, only to find her arms grabbed and held firmly by one of Carlos' men. Marsha's eyes gleamed, a look of triumph on her face.

"You belong to us now, Julia, to me and Carlos and anyone else who wants you."

"No!"

Calmly, Carlos lit a cigar, watching her carefully through the rising smoke.

"It's true. Nico is yesterday's man, a has-been, a loser."

Marsha released her hold on Julia's breast and moved to stand closer to Carlos.

"Believe him, Julia. My department can't turn a blind eye to the activities of every racketeer in town and my friends and I decided that our fortunes were best served by Carlos. That left Nico high and dry with nowhere to go, although he found somewhere fast enough when he heard we were stepping up our investigations."

Julia struggled to make sense of what she was being told. Obviously Nico had failed in his attempts to corrupt the new administration. If they were all like Marsha he had been wasting his time anyway because she was already corrupt and obviously an old hand at playing one party off against another. That left the question of what had actually happened to Nico of course, and more importantly, what was to happen to her.

"What... what have you done to him?"

"Nico? Are you really interested? Well, after we persuaded a number of his key men to throw in their lot with us and raided a few of his establishments he got the message and left town in a hurry. He really has nowhere to go except back to where he came from. I think he headed back to Columbia or Guatemala or somewhere like that."

Julia felt stunned at the speed at which Nico's empire seemed to have collapsed, but there was a greater shock still waiting for her. Carlos leaned back across his desk and pressed a button on the intercom before facing her once more, his smile broader than ever.

"That means of course that whatever or whoever Nico owned here in America, I now own and I even got myself a bonus."

The door swung open to the sound of a scuffle and Natalie was bundled roughly into the room, a hefty shove sending her sprawling on the floor. Her wrists were cuffed behind her back and her usually elegant clothes were torn and dirty but her temper was hot.

"You fucking bastard, Carlos! Nico will cut your throat for this!"

Carlos regarded her calmly, puffing on his cigar while she vented her temper on the room at large until she ran short of breath.

"My dear girl, as I've just finished explaining to Julia

here, your brother is in no position to cut the throat of anything more important than a chicken so please stop screaming and shouting or I'll have you gagged."

Breathing heavily, Natalie glowered up at him, his words very obviously confirming what she had already guessed.

"So you're the big man for now, Carlos. But one day..."

Carlos shrugged, amused at her show of defiance.

"Perhaps, but until then you'll be working for me and I'm sure you don't need it spelling out."

For a moment Natalie went pale and then her natural arrogance returned and she struggled to her feet, facing him squarely.

"Go to hell!"

"You are not in a position to bargain with me, Natalie."

"I won't be your whore and you can go to hell!"

Julia had been in similar situations before and knew exactly what would happen next. She watched with a kind of mesmerised fascination as two of Carlos' henchmen moved unobtrusively into position behind Natalie as she stood defiant. hands on hips.

Carlos nodded.

"Strip her!"

Too late, Natalie recognised the trap. Even as she turned around she was seized from behind, her arms pinned to her sides. Furiously she lashed out with her feet but the man holding her leaned heavily against her, his weight pushing her down onto her knees. His companion reached down for her, his hand sliding easily inside her already torn blouse and seconds later it was ripped from her body and cast aside. Her bra followed, the flimsy lace offering no resistance.

"Nice tits, honey. Maybe Mr Carlos will let me play with them later."

Julia glanced across at Carlos, shuddering slightly at the cruel glint in his eyes as he watched Natalie's humiliation. The sound of tearing cloth brought her attention back to the spectacle in front of her as Natalie's ruined skirt joined the pathetic heap on the floor. Only her brief lace panties remained and moments later they too were ripped disdainfully away, leaving her totally naked and vulnerable.

Julia knew how that felt and her heart went out to Natalie at being so lewdly and brutally exposed, but Carlos was far from finished with her.

"Now tie her legs to the desk. Nice and wide so we can all see what she's got."

Natalie struggled but her efforts were in vain as she was dragged to the desk and her ankles tied to the legs. One of the men began to press her forward but Carlos stopped him with a dismissive wave.

"Leave her standing. I want to watch her tits bouncing when Marsha whips her."

Natalie's shocked gasp was clearly audible, but everyone else grinned at the prospect. Julia was shocked herself, imagining the sudden tension and apprehension that Natalie must now be feeling. After an upbringing which allowed her to dispense punishments at will it was now her turn to feel the sting of the lash, and at the hands of Marsha of all people.

Marsha prolonged the tension, seating herself at the desk and opening a drawer to reveal an assortment of whips and canes which she proceeded to lay out as though for display. Natalie's gaze was drawn irresistibly down, her face growing paler with every new whip laid out before her, and Julia herself felt a kind of sick fascination as she too looked on, wondering which lash would be selected.

Julia's attention shifted back to Natalie again and again, her feelings a confused cocktail of eagerness to witness the thrashing and humiliation of her former mistress and pity at the young girl's helpless plight. She was certain that after Carlos and Marsha had finished with Natalie it would be her turn to submit to their whims, and yet she found herself able to accept that with a sense of calm detachment, so caught up was she in the spectacle unfolding around her.

Marsha made her choice, her hand settling on a slender horsewhip and Natalie visibly shuddered. It was obvious that she was now very frightened of what she knew was to come, her nipples tightly puckered and her legs shaking.

Julia had no need to look down to confirm that in contrast, she was becoming highly excited, her own nipples jutting proudly and tingling with arousal. Marsha glanced quickly in her direction, her smile signalling that she too recognised Julia's increasing state of arousal and then she picked up the whip and swished it through the air.

The effect on Natalie was immediate. Her eyes widened as she sucked in her breath. Her gaze was fixed on Marsha and Julia knew she was longing to be told how severe her thrashing was to be and wondering how she could possibly withstand the pain and humiliation.

"Whenever you're ready, Marsha, and don't bother with anything fancy. We just want to show the bitch who's the boss now."

Carlos slipped into the chair, watching Natalie very closely as Marsha stood up and walked slowly but purposefully round the desk. Despite the fact that she was not yet under punishment, Julia felt her heart beginning to beat harder and faster, a familiar dryness in her mouth as she waited for the first sharp crack of supple leather against soft yielding flesh.

Swish!
Thwack!
Swish!
Crack!

Natalie stiffened, her back arching sharply back as the lash cracked wickedly down. Her bare breasts bounced and her whole body quivered in response to the savage bite of the leather, but she managed to keep herself under control, her lips clamped shut against her instinctive gasp of pain.

Swish!
Crack!
Swish!
Crack!

Seeing her silence as a challenge, Marsha whipped the lash in harder and faster and even Julia jumped a little as the sound of the thrashing rang around the room. This time Natalie's resolve crumbled and she twisted and bucked wildly, a high pitched shriek following hard on each searing impact.

"That's more like it. I thought you were pussyfooting around for a while there, Marsha."

Natalie was breathing hard, bare breasts heaving, a sheen of perspiration glistening on her body as she twisted round desperately to see where the next blows would land.

Swish!
Crack!
Swish!
Thwack!

With even greater force, Marsha lashed at her unprotected flanks and Natalie howled out loud, tethered thighs smacking into the side of the desk as she writhed under the stinging, bruising punishment. Her trembling legs were unable to support her any longer and she pitched forward, breasts swinging down to brush against the polished top of the desk. With a startled cry she suddenly realised what she had done and struggled to drag herself upright once more.

Too late!
Swish!
Crack!
Swish!

Crack!

The force of the blows delivered full across her upthrust backside smacked her forward once more. The breath was driven from her body in an anguished howl as her heaving breasts bounced heavily against the desk and from now on there was no respite.

Thwack!
Thwack!
Thwack!
Thwack!

Marsha whipped in the lash relentlessly and Julia looked on dry mouthed and flinching with each ringing impact. Now that Natalie was bent right forward she could see the angry red welts criss crossing the young girl's backside, watch the desperate clenching and quivering of her buttocks as each new stoke whistled in. This was no mere whipping. This was a savage lesson in obedience. Julia knew from her plaintive cries that Natalie was learning her lesson from a harsh and unforgiving mistress. She glanced quickly at Marsha and Carlos, seeing the gleam of cruel excitement in their eyes and knew that this was only the first of many such lessons for Natalie, an enemy now in their power, a substitute perhaps for Nico.

Thwack!
Thwack!

"Enough! For now."

Marsha stepped back reluctantly as Carlos raised his hand, her own breasts heaving and her face glowing. Natalie lay across the desk, uttering small whimpering noises as tears ran freely down her cheeks, her buttocks still clenching and trembling even though her torment had ceased.

"Stand her up. Let me get a good look at her."

One of the men standing by moved quickly, hauling Natalie upright. Carlos reached out, thrusting his hand between her parted thighs without ceremony, fingers probing at her sex.

"Bitch is closed up real tight. She didn't like! What do you say, Natalie?"

Natalie could only moan in reply, flinching as Carlos transferred his attention to her breasts, pinching her still shrivelled nipples.

"Well you'd better just get used to it and real quick because I'm putting Marsha in charge of your training and I think she got a real kick out of thrashing your sweet little ass."

Everyone laughed as Marsha nodded in emphatic agreement and Carlos jerked his thumb dismissively at his men.

"Take her away guys and have yourselves a little fun, know what I mean?"

Beaming with delight the man holding Natalie bent to untie her ankles before dragging her sharply towards the door. Natalie sagged weakly and almost collapsed but the man supported her, his hands closing firmly around her heaving breasts.

"Come on honey and get to know some real men."

Everyone laughed again and Natalie cast a despairing glance back towards Carlos as she was hauled out of the room, her bottom glowing red and savagely striped as clear evidence of her suffering. Another hard and equally humiliating lesson lay ahead for her and Julia felt a stab of pity at the realisation of how utterly Natalie's safe and ordered world had collapsed around her, leaving her floundering in an endless nightmare.

As the door closed, Carlos switched his attention back to Julia. Marsha, too, smiled wickedly in her direction, the whip still trailing loosely from her hand.

Chapter Twenty One

For what seemed like an age, Carlos sat staring thoughtfully at Julia while Marsha hovered menacingly nearby, the whip still trailing loosely from her hand. Julia could see that she was obviously aroused as were both her lover and Carlos, both men making no attempt to conceal the bulges of their straining erections. The silence seemed almost physical and when Carlos at last spoke, she jumped as though startled.

"I guess you're about ready to get yourself fucked, Marsha, and from the look of Paul over there I guess he won't wait much longer."

"What about her?"

Marsha tossed her head in Julia's direction and Julia licked her lips nervously.

"You can leave her to me. It's time I had a little fun myself."

Marsha was obviously annoyed but she recovered her composure quickly as Paul rose eagerly from his chair.

"Well, I suppose I've had enough fun for one evening and I shouldn't be greedy."

Now that the chance of being allowed to exercise domination over Julia had been removed she seemed to lose interest. She moved over to Paul, reaching down to fondle him through his jeans, her expression suddenly impish.

"My, my, Paul, what have you got lurking in there?"

Taking his hand she headed for the door and Julia felt a surge of relief. She remembered how Paul made use of her at Marsha's house and permitted herself a brief smile as she wondered how long he would hold out this time. Hopefully it was now Marsha's turn to feel frustrated but for now there was the more urgent matter of what Carlos intended to do to her. She had no doubt that Carlos would whip her but somehow that seemed a less daunting prospect than submitting to Marsha. Indeed, having witnessed how savagely Marsha could mete out a punishment, she doubted if Carlos could flog her any harder despite him being a man.

Carlos remained silent until the door shut behind Marsha and Paul, and Julia knew better than to speak herself. The collection of straps and canes was still strewn about the desk where Marsha had left them and she wondered which of them Carlos would choose.

"Marsha frightens you, doesn't she?"

"A little."

Carlos chuckled.

"I think she frightens you a lot. What about me? Are you frightened of me?"

Julia hesitated, fearing a trap, but Carlos was watching her intently, waiting for an answer.

"Yes."

Carlos sorted idly through the whips and canes lying in front of him, noting how she couldn't quite conceal her differing reactions to each one he touched.

"Are you frightened by the fact that I'm going to whip you?"

Julia's mouth was suddenly dry and she nodded, her voice suddenly quiet.

"But I thought being whipped gave you a buzz and really turned you on?"

Julia shuffled nervously, well aware that Carlos already knew everything about her.

"I, yes, I can't help it."

"To hell with that. Does it turn you on or not?"

"Yes."

Julia hung her head, knowing that from now on things could only get worse.

"So when I whip you, with this cane perhaps, then you'll get aroused?"

Carlos was pressing the point, enjoying her discomfort as she struggled to find an answer that did not shame her even more.

"Yes, but..."

"Do you enjoy being aroused?"

"Yes, but..."

Carlos was ignoring her protests, and she stared hard at the floor, wishing he would just thrash her there and then without such an embarrassing preamble. He had obviously decided on the cane, a slender whippy rod which he was flexing carefully. She fought down the urge to shudder at the thought of its undoubtably cruel bite.

"So. Let me get this right. When I thrash your ass with this cane you'll get aroused and you'll enjoy being aroused, is that right?"

"No. I mean yes."

"Yes or no, which?"

Julia felt utterly trapped and helpless, knowing what he wanted from her but unable to bring herself to give in easily.

"Yes."

"Yes, what?"

"Yes, when you thrash me it'll turn me on."

"And you'll enjoy that?"

"Yes, yes, in the end..."

Julia hung her head even lower as Carlos closed the trap on her.

"Well then, Julia, if you're going to enjoy it so much I guess it wouldn't hurt if you asked me."

Julia closed her eyes and took a deep breath before facing him squarely, very aware now of the cane flexing between his hands.

"Please, Mr Carlos, I'd like you to beat me."

"Are you sure?"

"Yes. I want you to beat me."

"With this?"

Carlos brandished the cane and she felt her stomach lurch but there could be no going back.

"Yes, Mr Carlos, please beat me with that cane."

"If I beat you, Julia, I'll beat you hard. Is that what you really want?"

Julia squirmed. Things were going from bad to worse and she wished she was already bending over the desk or a chair or wherever he wanted her, rather than being made to beg in such a humiliating manner. She took another deep breath.

"Yes, Mr Carlos. I want you to beat me hard, as hard as you can."

She knew by now that whatever she said he intended to thrash her hard, but being made to ask for it sent her spirits plummeting. Carlos beamed his satisfaction and walked around the desk towards her, the cane hanging loosely in his grasp.

"Stand up properly."

Julia straightened up, clasping her hands behind her back and squaring her shoulders. Her breasts jutted proudly forward, nipples already firm and swelling even harder as she reacted to the prospect of being thrashed.

"Nice tits. I've heard that Marsha sometimes whips them."

Julia gasped out loud. Surely Carlos wasn't thinking about beating her breasts with the cane? She watched, fascinated as he raised it up, sliding the slender rod under the swell of her breasts as though to balance them. The wood felt hard and unyielding and she shuddered at the thought of it lashing down across her soft flesh.

Carlos slid the cane up around the swell of her breasts, steadying it under her nipples, and despite her fears she felt a tingle of excitement as he began to work it slowly back and forth, across the throbbing buds. Her breathing was deep and regular, but there was no disguising her mounting excitement as her nipples jutted out hard and solid from her breasts under the relentless stimulation.

Thwipp!

With a speed that caught her by surprise, Carlos lifted the cane and flicked it down across the curving slopes of her breasts. The blow did not cut into her but it stung dreadfully and she cried out, staggering back in a confusion of shock and pain. Her breasts heaved and shook, a dull red stripe darkening rapidly across the pale tan while tears sprang to her eyes.

Thwipp!

Carlos pursued her, laying the cane fully across the firm swell of her breasts once more, a fresh stripe darkening above her nipples. Again Julia howled out loud, twisting away from him as the sharp stinging flared through her. She could feel her body responding, her nipples swelling up so hard that she felt they could burst, while between her thighs she could feel her sex lips swelling too. She was totally confused, her breasts stinging from the two cuts of the cane she had endured and yet a feeling of deep excitement flooding through her.

She swung to face Carlos fully, thrusting out her breasts as though in defiance, her body trembling, but her spirit unbroken.

Thwipp!
Thwipp!

Her breasts shook as the cane whipped in, searing the softer flesh under her nipples and while she howled and writhed under the stinging strokes she could feel her body responding. Waves of arousal washed through her and her legs trembled as she staggered back once more.

Carlos was aroused too, his eyes fixed on the dull red stripes decorating her otherwise perfect breasts. He lowered the cane and reached out to fondle her and she whimpered softly as his fingers traced lightly over her bruised and throbbing flesh. Still locked within their confining rings, her nipples strained out, hard, hot and tingling. The merest touch of his hand was enough to send shocks rippling down into her belly.

She flinched and whimpered again as he traced along the deep red stripes under each nipple, but already the pain was becoming dulled, overlaid by her growing sense of arousal. Without conscious thought she leaned forward into him, pressing her heavy breasts harder against his exploring hands, moaning softly as her excitement mounted.

Thwipp!

She jumped back, yelping with surprise as Carlos flicked the cane across her flanks.

"I'm not finished with you just yet, Julia. You asked me to beat you hard, remember?"

Protest died away as she saw the eager glint in Carlos' eye. He wanted to beat her and there was no avoiding what lay ahead. Her shoulders sagged and she stared hard at the floor while he took a few practice swings, the cane whistling wickedly through the air. She longed to ask how many strokes she would be made to endure, but girls in her position were not invited to ask questions and in any case, he probably hadn't decided himself.

"Across the desk. Ass pushed well out."

This was familiar ground and Julia hurried across to the desk and the spot so recently occupied by the hapless Natalie. Suddenly mindful of her very swollen and tender nipples, she took a step back before leaning forward, her arms crossed along the edge of the edge of the desk, her head pillowed on top. Her back dipped towards the floor, her breasts swaying invitingly beneath her and her bottom presented a perfect target as it jutted out and up behind her.

Without needing to be reminded, she spread her thighs wide, drawing her buttocks into a smooth, tight curve and presenting Carlos with a clear view of her sex.

The position was familiar, her sense of submission absolute, and she felt her heart pounding, her whole body alive with the first spasms of arousal even though she was dreading the ordeal of the first few strokes of the cane across her unprotected behind.

She could have turned her head away, but instead she watched with barely suppressed excitement as Carlos walked slowly into position behind her, the cane now clenched very firmly in his fist. His eyes gleamed and his expression told her that he intended to lay into her as hard as he could.

She wasn't sure she could take it, even though she knew that she had no choice. Yet that very thought seemed to fuel her excitement. Her hips wriggled involuntarily, the tightly drawn cheeks of her backside jiggling from side to side.

Carlos smiled as he saw it.

"You can't wait, can you?"

She said nothing, watching as he stepped round behind her, out of sight. The room was very quiet, her heart pounding so hard that she was sure Carlos could hear and she concentrated on breathing deeply, bracing herself against the imminent onslaught. Carlos drank in the sight of her, prostrate and submissive, her breasts just visible as they dangled beneath her like inverted bells.

Slowly, he slid the tip of the cane between her parted thighs, lifting the slender rod to brush across the soft wet folds of her sex lips. Julia stiffened, sucking in her breath at the touch, and then as she realised what he was doing to her she wriggled her hips again, thrusting herself down onto the probing shaft.

The cane slipped easily between the parted folds of flesh, rubbing insistently across the hard bud of her clitoris. She wriggled again, sucking in her breath as Carlos increased the pressure, lifting his arm and bedding the cane deeper into her. He began to move it back and forth in a deliberate sawing motion, watching fascinated as she appeared to ride the slender rod. Her hips pumped steadily as she bore down on the wood, uncaring of the lewd display she was presenting as she pleasured herself.

The cane glistened wet with her freely flowing juices and a thin sheen of perspiration began to show on her body as her excitement mounted. Between her spread thighs her sex gaped, the lips quivering and twitching as though under the touch of some unseen lover. Her breasts swung in time to the thrusting of her hips, nipples jutting boldly out from the confining rings. She was losing control, her body alive with the thrill of arousal under the relentless stimulation of her tender flesh.

Low gasping moans escaped from her lips as Carlos lifted the cane higher, raising her up onto her toes. Her hips swayed from side to side, the taut, curved swell of her backside jutting out behind her.

Swish!

Thwack!

With one smooth movement, Carlos slid the cane from between her legs and brought it slashing down to connect full across those inviting cheeks. Her bottom quivered, the thin track where the cane had bitten into her flaring an angry red and Julia howled aloud at the sudden stinging impact.

Swish!

Thwack!

Swish!

Thwack!

Without giving her time to recover, Carlos whipped the cane in twice more, the smack of the wood against her pliant flesh ringing loud around the room. Julia bucked and heaved, her wildly clenching buttocks criss crossed with the searing welts. Her backside was on fire already, the speed and ferocity of the blows driving the breath from her body as she writhed under the onslaught.

Swish!

Whack!

The cane whistled in under the curve of her buttocks, lashing the tender flesh of her thighs and smacking into the gaping lips of her sex. Now she did cry out, a high keening wail escaping from her lips as the fierce pain ripped into her. Her hips twisted and heaved madly, her bottom swinging from side to side as though in an attempt to both evade the stinging blows and fan cooling air across her cruelly heated flesh.

Carlos stood back, his own chest heaving, his eyes alight as he watched her desperate struggles. He marvelled that she still held her submissive pose when every instinct in her body must be screaming at her to run and hide from the savage beating she was enduring.

He reached out to rest his hand on her punished backside, feeling the heat of the thrashing he had given her flaring through her tender flesh.

She whimpered, shuddering under his touch, buttocks clenching uncontrollably as his fingers traced along the angry weals. Between her thighs he could see her sex gaping wet and inviting, just as it had been when Marsha had tormented her for his amusement. His fingers slipped down along the wet folds of flesh and Julia whimpered again, lifting up onto her toes, her pulsating sex pressing urgently against his exploring hand.

Any time he wanted he could fuck her and he knew

now that despite the stinging welts striping her backside, she would respond eagerly. His eyes narrowed, a wicked smile stealing across his lips as he lifted the cane and brought it swinging down again.

Swish!
Whack!
Swish!
Whack!

Julia howled, her legs kicking wildly as the savage pain ripped through her already tortured backside. For a few brief moments while Carlos had fondled her she had let herself dare to believe that the thrashing was over. Her defences had dropped and now she sprawled forward under the onslaught, her swaying, bruised breasts banging painfully against the side of the desk.

Swish!
Whack!
Swish!
Whack!

Carlos kept up the punishing rhythm without giving her time to recover what little composure she retained. He smacked the cane up across the top of her thighs, raising her higher onto her toes. Tears smarted in Julia's eyes and her hips bucked and heaved beyond her control. Her backside was on fire and she doubted her ability to withstand any more punishment. Except that she had no choice. If she resisted in any way, Carlos would undoubtably call for his men to either hold her or tie her down while he completed the beating.

The realisation of her utter helplessness seemed to trigger perverse feelings deep inside her and as she writhed and squirmed under the relentless thrashing, she felt a first welcome wave of arousal washing through her belly.

Swish!
Thwack!

She gasped out loud as the cane cracked full across the taut swell of her upthrust buttocks, but now the wave of heat that swept through her punished behind spread out to enfold the swelling lips of her sex. Between her legs she could feel herself opening, a warm trickle of moisture bathing the soft skin of her inner thighs. She gasped again, thrusting her backside higher to receive the stinging strokes.

Swish!
Whack!
Swish!
Whack!

Her hips were bucking in a steady rhythm now, responding to the urgent desires building up inside her as her body at last responded to the beating. She cried out aloud, spreading her thighs wider, her sex gaping now in lewd invitation, the lips pulsating and quivering as though she was being penetrated by an unseen lover.

Her breasts swung heavily against the desk, sharp spasms rippling through her constrained nipples with each bruising contact. She was beyond caring. Her world was defined by the fiery pain lancing through her backside and the urgent throbbing of her nipples and her sex. Her body dripped perspiration and her breath rasped noisily in her throat as she thrust her hips up and back, offering herself shamelessly to be flogged.

Swish!
Thwack!

Carlos whipped another savage stroke across her tautly jerking buttocks, drawing a sharp cry from her lips and setting her twisting and writhing even more desperately. His eyes gleamed with lust, his face covered in a thin sheen of sweat and his erection pressed hard and urgent against his jeans. Dropping the cane, he fumbled with the zipper, tearing his jeans and shorts down his legs, his eyes never leaving Julia's bent and writhing body.

His cock sprang upright, jutting out long and thick from the coarse mat of hair at his groin, brushing against Julia's sore and abused backside as he reached for her. She cried out loud as he seized her around the waist, hauling her upright and spinning her round to face him, the sudden movement sending a stinging jolt through her well thrashed backside.

"You want it, don't you? You want me to fuck you?"

"Yes! YES!"

Julia's reply was husky, breathless, her body trembling as she faced him.

"Then say it, Julia. Say it out loud."

His hands were at her breasts, fingers fumbling clumsily at the catches of her nipple rings, his touch sending fresh spasms racing through her.

"Ahhhhh!"

The rings opened and her freed nipples throbbed and tingled almost unbearably.

"Ahhhhh!"

She staggered back, her buttocks bumping against the desk, inflaming the pain of the thrashing she had endured. For a few moments tears sprang to her eyes and then the underlying feeling of arousal surged through her once more. Carlos was at her at once, his hands moulded around her breasts as he pushed her steadily back.

"Say it, Julia!"

"Fuck me, fuck me, fuck me..."

He pushed her down onto her back across the desk, her hips dangling clear of the edge and without conscious thought she spread her legs wide to receive him.

"Say it again, Julia."

"Fuck me, Carlos, please... FUCK ME!"

Raising her head she peered down between her jutting, swollen breasts. She could see him clearly, his cock swaying between her thighs as he prepared to penetrate her. She licked her lips, spreading her legs wider, feeling herself opening for him. She imagined how she must look to him, her body hot and glistening with sweat, her breasts thrusting boldly up and the deep red gash of her sex gaping open between her thighs. Her hips twitched, lifting urgently towards him, her eyes pleading for his touch. She knew her behaviour was wanton, shameless, but she didn't care.

The hours of naked exposure, the constant fondling she had endured over dinner, the sight of Natalie being flogged into submission and, finally, the savage beating that Carlos had inflicted on her all combined to send waves of lust washing through her that only a cock thrusting deep into her sex could satisfy.

Carlos was filled with lust too, a burning need for release that had been growing inside him since he had been left alone with this luscious girl to treat her as he pleased. He entered her without finesse, ramming the thick, swollen length of his cock deep into her in one mighty thrust of his hips.

"Yessss!"

Julia's hips jerked up to meet him and she slid backwards across the polished surface of the desk until he bent forward to grab her, holding her still as he withdrew and thrust again. She could feel the last dregs of her control slipping away and surrendered herself to the tide of passion ripping through her, twisting in his grasp and crying out loud as his heavy cock reamed her dripping slit.

His grip shifted to her breasts and she arched her back, writhing and squirming in response to the sudden jolts of pleasure rippling out from her nipples. Her whole body was gripped by spasms of release, sweeping through her in wave after relentless wave.

She twisted and heaved, her breathing quick and ragged, her whole being centered on a narrow band of pleasure between her breasts and her belly. Carlos held her tight, riding her twisting belly, cock ramming in and out of her faster and faster as his climax approached.

She was sobbing out loud, not with pain but rather the sheer joy of sexual release. Each thrust of his cock inside her seemed to drive her on and as he looked down at the sheer wanton sight she presented, he felt his own orgasm gripping him. His hands clutched at her breasts, fingers tightening as he came, jetting thick, hot jets of sperm deep inside her and still she writhed beneath him. Her body was gleaming, slick with sweat and her hips ground ceaselessly against him, matching him thrust for thrust until at last he jetted the last of his sperm into her and fell forward across her breasts. For a while she continued to writhe beneath him and then her orgasms eased and she lay quiet and quivering, her heart pounding loud in his ears.

"Well, that sure was a real good fuck. I guess everything I've heard about you is true."

Julia said nothing, watching through half closed eyes as Carlos slipped out of her and reached for his clothes. She was still trembling in the aftermath of the orgasms that had racked her and didn't want to risk moving without being told. The mingled wetness of her own juices and the sperm leaking slowly out of her suddenly felt cold between her thighs and she shivered where she lay.

"Feeling cold?"

"A little."

Carlos smiled, zipping up his jeans and reaching for the intercom on the desk.

"Well, there's a warm bed waiting for you somewhere. I guess you've earned it."

He reached down to fondle her breasts for one last time before helping her to her feet and walking her to the door.

"I'd like you to think of yourself as my guest for the next few days, Julia."

"Thank you."

Her reply seemed inadequate, stupid even, considering what had just passed between the two of them, and then Carlos opened the door and a maid was waiting to take her to her room.

Chapter Twenty Two

Next morning Julia was summoned to breakfast with Carlos.

She was still stiff and sore and would really have preferred at least another hour in bed, but that was out of the question. The maid who had been given the task of looking after her made sure she was out of bed then left her alone as she showered, returning a few minutes later with her dress. It had been cleaned and pressed and Julia seized on it gratefully, relieved at the modesty it afforded her even though everyone in the house would know that she was naked underneath.

She wondered briefly how Natalie had fared during the night, and then dismissed the girl from her thoughts. Nico was obviously finished and after the events of the previous evening, Natalie was in no position to help herself, never mind Julia: it was a case of every woman for herself.

She followed the maid to a small outside terrace where Carlos was breakfasting alone. The table was littered with the morning papers. If she had any doubts that he had told her the truth about Nico's misfortune, the headlines dispelled them. Paper after paper led with the raids against his fallen empire and speculation regarding his current whereabouts.

She wondered what Carlos intended to do with her and was surprised when he suddenly smiled broadly and pulled out a chair for her, calling to the maid to bring some more food.

"Full English breakfast, Julia, just to make you feel at

home."

She sat carefully, mindful of how sore her bottom still was from the thrashing he had given her.

"Still a little tender, huh?"

"Just a little."

She forced a smile, expecting him to order her to stand up and raise her dress to show him, but already he was back to leafing through the papers.

"Hurry up in there, guys, we're both starving to death out here."

He smiled again and she realised how hungry she was as his men brought heaped platefuls of food to the table. Carlos tucked in at once and Julia followed his example, much to his approval.

"Breakfast has to be the best thing to come out of your country, Julia, except maybe for you."

She blushed, still wondering what he had in mind for her and was taken by surprise at his next announcement.

"I'm making arrangements to have you sent back there, Julia."

She stared at him dumbstruck, a forkful of bacon frozen half way to her mouth.

"You can take your money and your clothes and I'll be sorry to see you go but it's probably for the best."

"But... I thought..."

Her voice trailed away as the implications of what she was being told sunk in. She had expected nothing to change for her except that now it would be Carlos who would be her boss instead of Nico. She had even been prepared to be told that Carlos wasn't going to pay her as generously as Nico, if indeed he was intending to pay her anything at all. His calm announcement however was so completely unexpected that she was lost for words and totally confused.

"You expected I would make you work for me the way Natalie's going to, right?"

"Well, yes..."

"It wouldn't work, Julia. It wouldn't work because you don't like the people you would have to work with. Am I right?"

Julia sat and thought about Marsha and her lover, about Bob and Mike and who knew how many other perverted and sadistic officials parading under the false banner of moral decency she might be required to satisfy in the months and years ahead and knew he was right.

"Yes."

Her voice was barely a whisper. She had thought it out this far herself yesterday afternoon, even taking the first hesitant steps towards building herself a new life and now Carlos was handing it to her on a plate. Carlos nodded, his expression momentarily serious.

"See, you already know that yourself and I'm afraid that if I force you to go on satisfying them you'll get to the point where you'll really have had enough and want out of the whole deal, no matter how much I pay you. The danger then is that you'll want to bring someone down with you by selling your story to the press and that's a risk I can't afford to take."

"I wouldn't do that!"

"Maybe not, but it's not worth the risk. Far better that I send you home now."

Julia realised that he was telling her that from now on no-one had a hold over her, not even Marsha. Relief flooded through her until uncertainty gripped her again.

"But..."

"But what?"

"What will I do?"

"You're rich enough. Don't worry about it."

"I mean what will I do about... oh, I don't know."

She sank back in her chair, thoroughly confused, and Carlos nodded thoughtfully.

"I see. You need to belong to someone... someone who'll beat you a lot, treat you the way you need."

She nodded tentatively.

"Maybe... but I just don't know."

Carlos looked at her for a few moments, a sympathetic smile on his face.

"I'll tell you what, stay here for a few days to think things over and in the meantime I'll make a call or two and see if I can come up with anyone who needs someone with your special talents. It shouldn't be too difficult."

Julia looked at him, her expression suddenly wary.

"What if I don't like him. Or her?"

Carlos shrugged to indicate that wasn't a problem.

"Nobody owns you, Julia, it'll be your choice all the way."

Chapter Twenty Three

Marsha appeared to take the news of Julia's impending departure quite calmly, agreeing with Carlos that it was probably for the best.

She had Natalie's training to attend to in any case and Julia got the distinct impression that she found great satisfaction in breaking the will of that proud and stubborn young woman.

Indeed, her whole attitude to Julia seemed to change for the better. Julia had been getting by on the dress in which she had arrived and an assortment of clothes borrowed from one of the maids and now Marsha actually suggested she should visit her old apartment to collect some suitable clothes.

Carlos allocated her a car and detailed Joe to drive her into town. This made her a little uneasy, but Joe made no mention of their previous encounter as she stepped out onto the drive.

There were two cars parked in front of the house and he was lounging against the one nearest the door and reached out smartly to open the rear door for her.

"Nice day for a run into town."

"Yes..."

She even managed a smile, but as she bent to climb into the car Joe grabbed her, pulling her off balance. She struggled instinctively against him but he was too strong for her, pinning her arms behind her back and slamming her hard against the side of the car.

The impact winded her and as she sagged weakly and

gasped for breath she felt the familiar cold touch of metal about her wrists as a pair of cuffs were snapped into place behind her back.

"Just a little precaution to make sure you don't try to run off or something equally silly."

She twisted round at the sound of Marsha's voice, her mind a sudden turmoil of confusion and anxiety. Marsha was watching her closely, a wicked smile on her lips.

"Don't worry, Julia. Just get in the car and settle down."

Julia felt far from reassured but had no choice other than to climb into the back of the car and sit still while Joe fastened her seat belt.

He lingered far longer than was necessary over the task, running his hands insolently over her breasts as he tightened the belt until despite herself she could feel her nipples beginning to swell.

Joe could feel them too and only an impatient reminder from Marsha prevented him from reaching inside her blouse to fondle her bare breasts.

"I'll drive this car, Joe, so stop playing with Julia's tits and go and help Wes."

"Yes, Miss Masterman."

Joe's face showed his disappointment but he ducked out of the car at once and went back into the house.

Now Julia was intrigued, and as she watched Joe returned in company with Wes and between them, looking weary but still defiant, was Natalie!

Julia could see that she was dressed in a similar blouse and skirt and her wrists also were cuffed firmly behind her. She still held her head high and proud, lowering it only to duck down into the back of the second car, and Julia imagined Joe's hands now roaming over Natalie's breasts as he fastened her seat belt.

The thought sent an unwanted tingle pulsing through Julia's nipples and she couldn't stop looking across at the other car and the shadowy movements behind the windows until once again Marsha called out impatiently to the two men.

"Come on. There'll be plenty of time for that later, you randy bastards."

Both men laughed and as Joe settled himself in the back alongside Natalie and Wes climbed into the driver's seat, Marsha slipped behind the wheel of the car containing Julia and started the engine.

Julia knew better than to ask questions, but it was obvious they were heading into the city. As the streets slipped past she recognised the neighbourhood and realised where Marsha was taking her.

Sure enough, a few minutes later, both cars pulled up outside Ricky's gym and Julia felt a deep sense of foreboding. The area looked as run down as ever, dirty rubbish-strewn streets and small groups of men hanging idly around each corner.

The nearest group regarded the arrival of the two cars with curiosity before returning once more to the more interesting occupation of drinking beer, and Marsha half turned to face Julia.

"I understand from Carlos that you feel a little dissatisfied with your situation, Julia."

Julia avoided her gaze, feeling more and more uneasy with every passing moment.

"He tells me that you feel you've been mixing with some real low life types and that you want a change."

Again Julia said nothing and Marsha grinned wickedly. "Well, I'm going to give both you and Natalie the chance of seeing what low life really is."

Turning to face front again, she pressed the horn sharply to catch the attention of the group at the nearest corner and Julia felt her stomach lurch as one of the men strolled casually across.

"You want something, lady?"

Marsha gestured to the car behind to make sure the man understood she was well protected. "My friends and I were wondering if you guys get to go with many good looking girls?"

"Us? Are you kidding, lady? We got diaries so full you wouldn't believe it - and every broad straight out of Hollywood!"

He threw back his head and laughed, revealing a mouth full of broken and yellowing teeth. Even in the back of the car Julia could smell the stale beer and her stomach lurched again.

"So you wouldn't be interested in servicing two hot little bitches for a couple of hours?"

"What! What's the angle?"

The man was taken by surprise and he glanced quickly at the second car before turning his attention back to Marsha.

"No angles, no questions, no comebacks. I've got two randy sluts who need a damn good seeing to! The rougher the better! Are you and your friends up to the job?"

The man was speechless.

"They'll be waiting in the gym. Come in ten minutes."

He gulped. "Right... well... yeah... sure thing, lady." He leered at Julia and her stomach lurched so violently she thought she was going to be sick. With her hands cuffed and the seat belt fastened tight she had no choice but to wait as Marsha climbed from the car and strode purposefully into the gym.

Joe yanked open the door and unlocked the belt, grabbing her and hauling her out onto the sidewalk before she had a chance to struggle.

His hand clamped like a vice around her arm and as he hustled her quickly along she heard a chorus of jeers and catcalls from the men at the corner. The calls became louder as they caught sight of her pinioned wrists.

Ahead of her, Natalie was being hustled through the door and Joe grinned wickedly as he cast a quick glance over his shoulder.

"The word's really going around!"

Julia knew that without looking. She could see more men hastening across the street, attracted by the commotion and she knew with a heart stopping certainty that they too would be allowed into the gym.

It was a relief to get off the street, but as Joe hustled her down the corridor she was aware of the men crowding round the door behind her. Their bodies blocked out the light and cutting off any chance of escape. Another chorus of jeers rang out and Joe grinned again as he bent down to thrust his face closer.

Julia shuddered as Joe shouldered open the door to the gym and bundled her inside.

To her great relief there was no sign of Ricky, only Wes and Marsha, lounging casually against the apparatus.

Natalie knelt on the floor. There was an air of defeat about her. She had obviously guessed what lay ahead and her eyes were wide with shock and fear.

Even when Julia was pushed to the floor beside her she barely noticed. Her attention was fixed on Marsha, her tongue darting out to moisten her lips again and again.

Marsha played on her anxiety and dragged out the waiting, delving into her handbag to extract a hundred dollar bill and handing it to Wes.

"It could be a long, hot afternoon, Wes, send one of those men to buy enough beer for everyone and bring it back here before we make a start."

"Sure thing, Miss Masterman." Wes went back outside and a few moments later there came a loud chorus of approval.

Julia imagined the effect the beer would have on the

men and shuddered again.

Alongside her, Natalie shuddered too, obviously sharing her thoughts, but neither girl dared utter a word as Marsha paced easily up and down the gym and the minutes dragged slowly by.

At last, Marsha checked her watch and snapped her fingers at Wes and Joe.

"Showtime, gentlemen and time for these two sluts to show what they've got to offer."

Both men grinned and closed in on the two kneeling girls and Julia swallowed hard. Without giving her a chance to move by herself, Joe grabbed her arm again and hauled her to her feet. His fingers tore at the buttons on her blouse, opening it fully to reveal her breasts before spinning her around and stripping the garment off her shoulders.

With her wrists cuffed he couldn't remove it completely, but left it pulled part way down her arms, laying her bare from the waist up.

Julia could see Wes stripping Natalie in an equally rough and ready fashion. The young girl's breasts bounced enticingly as he yanked the blouse hard down against her cuffs.

"The skirt too, Miss Masterman?"

His hand was thrust down the waistband, ready to rip the fastening open but Marsha shook her head.

"Not yet. We don't want the guys outside to get the idea that these two are totally shameless."

Everyone laughed except for Julia and Natalie.

Julia knew only too well what was coming and Natalie's imagination was working overtime. She crowded close to Julia as if to seek some meagre protection but Julia had nothing to offer.

Joe was opening the door and already she could hear the men jostling and pushing as they crowded the narrow corridor. Her heart was pounding madly and she could barely control the trembling in her legs as she waited, eyes fixed on the door through which they would pour in an excited stream and then the front runners entered the room and pandemonium broke out.

The sight of both girls stripped to the waist, bared breasts so brazenly on display, halted the first men in their tracks, bringing an immediate outbreak of pushing and cursing as those at the rear tried to force a way through. For a while it seemed likely that a fight would break out but at last everyone managed to squeeze through the door to stand open mouthed and leering at the sight.

Julia's heart pounded even more loudly as she counted more than a dozen men, all of them scruffy and dishevelled and all doubtless in dire need of a bath, but all of them, without exception, gazing at her bared breasts with undisguised lust. She saw Joe locking the door behind them and felt suddenly thankful that no more could enter, despairing already at the thought of the ordeal ahead.

Alongside her she could hear Natalie whimpering softly and felt a brief stab of pity. At least she had some experience of what was coming, while for Natalie this could only be the stuff of her worst nightmares.

"Don't fight it Natalie. You'll only make things worse if you do."

She wasn't sure if Natalie heard her whispered advice but at least she'd tried to help and now it was every girl for herself.

The men were fanning out, enclosing both girls in a wide circle and Julia scanned them quickly, wondering which of them would be the first to grab her. Her skin crawled at the thought of their hands on her breasts and she wished they would move in on her now, drag her to the floor and break the awful tension.

"You - the blonde! Come here!"

She turned to face the man who had spoken, fighting back her disgust as the smell of so many unwashed bodies engulfed her.

"I said, come here!"

There was an angry edge to his voice and Julia took a hesitant step forward.

"Move!"

A violent shove sent her stumbling forward and as she struggled to keep her balance the man reached out and grabbed her breast. His hands were rough and calloused, fingers digging into her firm flesh as he pulled her closer.

On all sides she could hear coarse shouts and laughter then her face was right up against his and she could smell the stale wine on his breath.

"The fancy dame over there says you need a good fucking, honey and that's just what you're going to get."

He pushed her back into the arms of his friends and tugged urgently at the zipper of his torn jeans, eyes already shining with lust. "You two get her panties off and I'll give her a ride she won't forget."

There were more shouts of laughter and Julia cringed as she felt one of the men holding her fumbling up under her skirt.

"She's not wearing any!"

"What?"

"Panties, man!"

As if in proof, the man yanked up her skirt and Julia cringed again. The sight of her smooth shaven sex prompted even greater excitement and now she could see a group closing in on Natalie and hauling up her skirt to see if she too was bare.

Licking his lips in anticipation, the man facing her reached out to grab at her sex, squeezing her hard until she was forced to bite her lip to avoid crying out. At the same time, the two men holding her began to fondle her, rough skinned palms cupping her breasts and sliding eagerly over her nipples. They began to swell at once as her body reacted to the unwanted but persistent stimulation. Her sex was squeezed again and she shuddered, moaning softly as the familiar feeling of sexual arousal began to claim her.

Her nipples throbbed, pinched tight now between bony fingers and swelling so hard she felt they would burst.

Between her thighs she felt thick fingers probing into her, opening her wide, thrusting deeper until she was unable to hold back any longer and gasped out loud.

It didn't matter any more who was preparing to fuck her. All that mattered was her body's urgent need for release as she writhed against the hands holding her captive.

"Over here... get her over here."

She was half dragged half carried across the gym towards a vaulting horse. Leering excited men crowded in on her. Eager hands grabbed her, lifting and pulling her into position. Her pinioned wrists were jammed into the small of her back, lifting her belly high. Rough hands pulled at her legs and shoulders, bending her back into a tight arc, breasts and belly jutting up and out. Her thighs were yanked wide apart and held tight, exposing her in the most obscene manner.

Her head hung down and in the press of bodies around her she could see nothing but she knew what was coming.

Her belly quivered and she tensed at the first probing thrust of a cock against the dragged open lips of her sex, then it was rammed inside her, penetrating deep, thrusting hard.

She gasped out loud, lifting her hips to meet him as the last of her reserves slipped away. It suddenly no longer mattered that the man fucking her was a dirty, unshaven tramp. All that mattered was the rush of arousal, the glorious feeling of being filled by a hard, thrusting cock.

She cried out loud, shuddering and squirming against the restraining hands, buttocks bouncing on the unyielding leather.

Around her she could hear the cries of encouragement, directed not at her but at the man fucking her so enthusiastically. A familiar madness swept through her as though she too shared in the wild excitement and she surrendered herself to the urgent demands of her body.

The men holding her down grabbed at her heaving breasts, clutching urgently at her, uncaring of her feelings, unable to contain their excitement as they waited their turn with her.

She knew they would all come quickly. Already she could feel the cock impaling her beginning to jerk wildly, the first thick jets of sperm spurting deep into her vagina while the man gasped and shuddered between her thighs.

She trembled on the brink of orgasm, moaning in despair as he slipped out of her. Then his place was taken by another. His thick cock slammed urgently into her and set her writhing once more.

One man straddled her, his erect cock thrusting arrogantly from his jeans and swaying above her face as he leaned forward to fondle her breasts.

The stale, unwashed smell of him filled her nostrils but the sight of his cock attracted her like a magnet and she strained up to reach it with her lips.

Too late!

Even as she parted her lips she saw him beginning to jerk forward as the excitement proved too much for him. His hands clutched her breasts, squeezing so hard that she cried out in pain and his cock jerked and twitched, spraying hot streams of sperm over her face.

It was enough to trigger her own orgasm, her body arching even tighter over the horse as the spasms gripped her. Her vagina tightened around the cock jammed so deep inside her and her hips bucked and heaved against the hands holding her down as wave after wave of release rippled through her captive body.

She heard herself gasping and moaning. The room blurred in a mist of sweat, then the man inside her came in a rush of hot sticky sperm, each spurt triggering a new shock through her belly.

Another man took his place, then another and another but all she knew was the shattering series of orgasms that gripped her again and again.

Her vagina was pumped so full of sperm that thick streams spurted out onto her thighs each time she was penetrated. Her nipples were so swollen and tender that she almost screamed each time they were touched.

Between her lips she could taste the semen of the man who had spent himself over her face as it trickled down into her mouth. Her whole body was hot and drenched with sweat and she ached all over but still the orgasms gripped her until at last there was no man left to claim her.

The hands holding her down lifted free and she slid to the floor, legs giving way beneath her to pitch her onto her knees. Her head spun and her body trembled uncontrollably, breasts heaving as she gasped for breath.

The men were crowding noisily into one corner of the gym and she remembered the beer they had bought. They had used her and left her but once rested and filled with beer they would be back.

Chapter Twenty Four

Julia shivered as the sweat dried on her naked body.

Somewhere along the way she had lost the meagre covering of her skirt. She could see it lying in a crumpled heap a few yards away from where she knelt, although she had no recollection of it being stripped away.

Natalie was naked too, lying on the floor, her body slick with sweat and patterned with angry red blotches where the men had pawed roughly at her. Her eyes were tight closed and only the rapid heaving of her breasts betrayed the fact that she was still conscious.

At one end of the gym the men were clustered in a noisy group, swigging beer and comparing the merits of the two girls in the crudest terms. Occasionally one of them would glance in their direction and gesture obscenely before laughing and turning back to the crowd with an even cruder comment.

Julia shivered again.

Her thighs were cold and wet from the semen oozing steadily from her sex and she longed for the chance to take a shower. The feelings of arousal that had sustained her through her ordeal had ebbed away and now she found herself dreading the moment when the men felt recovered enough to start in on her again.

It seemed as though that moment was closer than she feared for already, one of the men was detaching himself from the group and walking purposefully towards her.

It was the man who had fucked her first and who seemed to have appointed himself as leader for she noticed all the others had turned to watch.

"On your feet... you too, honey."

He reinforced his order by giving Natalie a none too gentle kick on the thigh as he passed, his face creasing into a grin at her yelp of protest.

No such persuasion was necessary for Julia. She was on her feet before he reached her and he nodded his approval.

"Like a drink?"

Julia suspected a trick but nodded anyway and he held up the can he was carrying.

"Open wide."

Obediently she opened her mouth, tipping back her head as he upended the can and released a stream of cold beer. The liquid splashed onto her face and ran down into her mouth and she gulped it down greedily, the excess beer spilling down her chin and cascading over her up tilted breasts.

"Here, honey... you too."

He gestured Natalie closer until she was standing side by side with Julia, moving the can back and forth above their raised faces until it was empty.

"The fancy dame over there says you can both go another session but some of the guys aren't quite ready yet, if you know what I mean?"

He gestured down at the half erect cock hanging insolently from his jeans and grinned broadly.

"So... I think it would be a real good idea if you two sluts put on a little show. You know the sort of thing I mean. Something to get us in the mood."

Julia nodded.

She understood very well what kind of show he wanted and from the corner of her eye she could see Natalie gasping with shock as understanding dawned on her.

"Yeah, I see you catch on fast... and you can lick each other clean at the same time."

He laughed out loud at the sick expression stealing over Natalie's face and grinned at Julia.

"Your friend doesn't seem too keen. Is she up to it?"

"She'll be fine." What else could she say?

"Hey Matt, you going to spend all afternoon just talking to those two or are we going to see some action?"

"Coming guys."

He thrust his face close, glaring hard, his eyes menacing. "Better make sure she is fine, the guys are looking forward to the show."

He beckoned them to follow him and Natalie edged closer to Julia, her face pale.

"I can't do it."

"You'd better, or they'll think of something worse."

Natalie shuddered, her face growing even paler. "It's all right for you....you love this kind of treatment."

"Not this kind of treatment, Natalie! It's as bad for me as it is for you but we have no choice. Play along or things will get worse, believe me."

The men were gathering into a wide semi circle and Matt directed both of them to stand in the middle where everyone could get a good view. In the background Julia could see Marsha with her two minders leaning back against the wall, her eyes shining with wicked delight as she watched the humiliating proceedings. She caught Julia's eye and smiled in triumph and Julia felt she had never hated anyone as much as she turned her attention back to Matt.

"You there, on the floor... and you, the blonde, get on top of her."

For a second it seemed as though Natalie was going to refuse then with a resigned shrug she settled herself on the floor. Without needing to be told she raised her knees and parted her thighs wide to give everyone a clear view of her ravaged sex and Matt nodded his grudging approval.

"Guess maybe I was wrong about her... now you."

Julia straddled Natalie, lowering herself carefully to kneel astride her breasts. Her shackled wrists made it awkward to lean forward without toppling off balance but she shuffled herself carefully into position until her lips were poised just above Natalie's sex.

"Lift up a little. We can't see your friend's tits."

Obediently, Julia straightened her thighs, the pose pitching her face further down towards Natalie's belly. Natalie's sex lay open beneath her, the lips red and swollen and smeared wetly with thick trails of sperm. Her nostrils filled with the mingled, musky odours of male and female arousal and she felt a pulse of desire beginning to beat inside her.

Her tongue darted out to lick quickly around the parted flesh, the salty taste of the sperm strong in her mouth as she bent closer.

Behind her she could feel Natalie straining up towards her own gaping and sperm spattered slit and the pulse of desire beat stronger. On numerous occasions she had pressed her lips to Natalie's sex, feeling the young woman opening beneath her but never so publicly and never with Natalie pleasuring her at the same time. Desire engulfed her and she thrust her mouth down on Natalie's sex, tongue spearing deep inside the dripping pit. Her breasts swayed softly against Natalie's belly, nipples hardening as they brushed over her smooth skin.

The young girl shifted beneath her, moaning softly, and then she too was busy at Julia's slit, tongue reaming deep inside her, lips closing firmly around the parted folds of flesh. Julia pitched further forward, sucking as much of Natalie as she could between her lips. Her mouth filled with a flood of sperm and she swallowed hard, gagging and choking a little as she forced it down.

Between her own wide spread thighs she could feel Natalie working on her, hesitant at first then bolder, rougher, her lips clamped firm and sucking hard while her tongue delved deep. Her belly quivered, exquisite shocks rippling through her with each intimate penetration, her gasps and moans muffled in the wet folds of Natalie's sex. Natalie was moaning too, her hips lifting, buttocks bouncing off the floor as Julia roused her.

The circle of watching men was forgotten, the crude comments and cries of encouragement ignored as both girls shuddered and gasped in the throes of rapidly mounting arousal.

The sharp tang of sperm in Julia's mouth was overlaid with the sweeter, muskier taste of woman and she knew Natalie's climax was close. Her own sex pulsed wetly between Natalie's lips, her nipples throbbing urgently against Natalie's belly as she bore down hard on the young girl's questing tongue. Her own tongue lashed at Natalie's tender flesh, driving her on, the writhing of her hips becoming more and more frenzied until she was heaving and squirming beyond control.

"Enough! That's enough!"

Julia yelped with pain and protest as her hair was twisted, pulling her away from the quivering pit of Natalie's sex. Another sharp tug and she fell forward, sex wrested free from Natalie's lips.

Matt held her tight, dragging her head back to see the throbbing erection jutting out from his jeans.

"Time for some real action, honey. Time to get those lips around this."

She needed no urging.

Her desire and arousal were so all consuming she would have taken anyone. Even the stale, unwashed smell of him failed to register as she reached eagerly for him. Not even the eager faces crowding close round deterred her as she darted out her tongue to lick once around the straining shaft before sucking it between her lips.

It was thick and stretched her lips wide, bulging her

cheeks out as she sucked it deep into her mouth. Between her spread thighs she could feel Natalie being pulled clear then there was only her and the man and the throbbing shaft jammed deep inside her mouth.

He was very aroused. His fingers gripped her hair tightly. His legs were already beginning to tremble as he pushed urgently against her. She struggled against his hold on her, letting him slip almost free of her lips as she gasped for breath. He snarled menacingly then realised what she was doing and relaxed his grip as he felt her tongue sliding wetly along the length of his cock.

With his cock stuffed once more between her lips, Julia's agreement sounded as nothing more than a muffled grunt and everyone laughed out loud.

Julia didn't care. She was caught up in the familiar feeling of being used for the pleasure of others and being able to do nothing to prevent it. It was a feeling that aroused her like no other and already she could feel the first tremors of orgasm rippling up through her belly. Rough hands roamed freely over her body, fondling her breasts and buttocks. Fingers probed between her thighs, sliding wetly along the gaping slash of her sex.

The press of bodies around her was almost suffocating, the heat and smell engulfing her. She shuddered and heaved, her body alive with arousal, her gasps and moans stifled by the cock thrusting steadily between her lips. A spasm gripped her then another and another, wave after wave of release ripping through her as Matt's cock exploded into her throat.

Swallowing hard, she took it all, barely aware of the taste of him filling her mouth as her orgasm claimed her. Her eyes misted over and her body shook. The confining press of men and the persistent groping and fondling seemed to intensify the spasms that racked her. Sweat drenched her body, dripping from her breasts and pooling between her thighs.

Her hips jerked back and her sex quivered and contracted tight around the fingers penetrating her, drawing them deeper inside and triggering new and stronger spasms in her belly. As Matt spent himself and pulled free of her lips she cried out aloud, her breasts heaving as she gasped for breath. The mist cleared from her eyes and she saw another cock, hard and throbbing already pressing towards her lips.

Through a gap in the crowd she saw Natalie lying on her back, her legs spread and bent back against her breasts. Two men were fondling her breasts while another fucked her vigorously. Her eyes were squeezed shut, her mouth gasping wordlessly as she too was racked by orgasms. Then the gap closed and her attention turned to the cock pressed urgently against her lips.

"Suck me, girl! Suck me good!"

Julia did, sucking him deep into her mouth and bringing him to a shattering climax that left her choking and gasping as his sperm jetted into her throat. His place was taken by another and then another and she satisfied them all. Unseen hands fondled her constantly, pulling at her engorged nipples, opening up her vagina and thrusting up into her to keep her writhing and heaving with arousal.

Her body glistened with a sheen of sweat, her breath rasping in her throat as orgasm after orgasm ripped through her. Thin trails of sperm dribbled from her lips and dripped stickily onto her breasts as she sucked on cock after cock in a relentless rhythm. She could feel her heart pounding madly, her head spinning from the rush of orgasm that engulfed her again and again.

Another jet of sperm spurted into her mouth, the cock slipping from between her lips and she groped forward blindly to find nothing. The last man had been satisfied and they were finished with her.

She shuddered and gasped, breasts quivering as the last spasms gripped her. Her knees gave way beneath her and she slid slowly to the floor, exhausted and still shaking. A few feet away she could see Natalie still lying on her back, her body twitching and shaking as she too fought herself back under control.

Marsha's heels clicked on the hard floor as she strolled over to inspect them more closely. Her eyes gleamed with wicked triumph but there was also a grudging respect for the two girls lying so spent and exhausted at her feet. There was no way either of them could take any more and she knew better than to force them.

"Alright you guys. show's over."

There was a chorus of protest but the sight of the cases of beer yet to be drunk, together with the sight of both Wes and Joe taking up an aggressive stance near the door proved enough to get them back onto the street.

"Right, you two, get them cleaned up and let's get out of here."

Marsha bent to unlock the cuffs and both girls were dragged to their feet and hustled into the changing room. The shower was as cold as Julia remembered, taking their breath away as they scrubbed themselves clean while Wes and Joe looked on in amusement.

The skirts and blouses they had worn on arrival were torn and crumpled but offered a welcome degree of modesty as the cuffs were fastened back in place before they were hustled outside and into the waiting cars.

The crowd of down and outs was gathered around the corner, a pile of empty beer cans littering the sidewalk and Julia's last impression was of their jeers and catcalls ringing out as the car door closed behind her.

Chapter Twenty Five

Julia spent the week that followed in an agony of indecision.

Natalie had been taken away to continue her 'training' at Marsha's country house and Carlos was occupied with his interests in the city, leaving her alone for much of the day. She had expected him to succumb to the temptation she presented by whipping her or at least fucking her again, but he seemed too preoccupied with consolidating his new found position of power and influence.

True to his promise he had made some telephone calls among his business associates and as another weekend approached he announced that she was to expect a visitor. A certain Charles de Vere, English like herself but with substantial interests in Florida and the Caribbean, had expressed great interest in meeting her with the possibility of asking her to work for him and Carlos had invited him to stay for a few days.

Julia had no illusions about what kind of duties she would be expected to perform, but she was still so undecided about her future and so frustrated by her period of idleness that she found herself quite looking forward to de Vere's arrival. She was both curious about the man himself and very interested indeed at the likelihood of him taking her to live in such an exotic place as the Caribbean.

She spent the time until his arrival fantasising about bright blue seas and endless golden beaches drenched in tropical sunshine and determined to make a good impression on him even if he did not measure up to her expectations.

He arrived home with Carlos and when Julia was introduced to him before dinner her first impression was of a tall, tanned and handsome man, barely forty years old and very well spoken. His English accent sounded calm and cultured after the brash American tones she had become accustomed to and she felt herself warming to him immediately.

Even more impressive was the fact that while he understood fully why he was meeting her and knew that she understood too, he made no attempt to lay claim on her.

All three of them talked and drank until late in the evening and that night she slept alone, racked with frustration and desire until she was driven to find relief in masturbation.

The next day, too, he kept his distance, questioning her about herself and how she had come to find herself in her present position. She answered all of his questions, holding nothing back until at last he held up his hand.

"I think I get the picture, Julia, and I think it's time we got to know each other a little better."

She nodded weakly, her legs suddenly shaking as she followed him to his room. With the door firmly locked and the curtains drawn against the bright afternoon sunshine he motioned her to sit on the bed while he switched on the television. Julia looked on puzzled as he put a cassette into the video recorder. She wondered briefly if his interests included pornographic movies. Perhaps he produced or directed or maybe even acted in them and was expecting her to act in them too. She wasn't sure how she felt about that and then the screen cleared and she gasped aloud as she saw herself, naked, and standing in front of the desk in Carlos' study!

There must have been a video camera, maybe a security camera, recording every detail of what had passed between Carlos and herself on the night she had been brought to see him. The picture was sharp and clear and she watched in a mixture of shame and fascination as the scene was played out in full. Nothing was missing.

She watched Carlos flicking the cane across her breasts before ordering her to prostrate herself over the edge of his desk. She watched herself bending forward submissively, her pose hiding nothing from his gaze as he stood eagerly behind her. She flinched as she watched the savage blows cracking down across her defenceless backside, the long welts showing dark against her skin while she writhed helplessly.

Last of all she felt her cheeks burning with embarrassment as she watched Carlos fucking her where she lay while she writhed beneath him, not with pain but with the sheer force of her orgasm. The screen flickered and went blank as the video ended and Charles turned to face her.

"Were you faking any of that, Julia?"

"Oh no. It was very real."

Her mouth was dry and she could feel her heart pounding as he stood up and walked towards her. She stood up too, her legs suddenly hardly even able to support her weight. She could see he was aroused, the bulge at his crotch very prominent, and she licked her lips as he placed his forefinger under her chin, tilting her face to his.

"I need to see for myself."

She nodded, feeling the first stirrings of arousal in her belly as he dropped his hands to his waist and began to remove his belt.

"I'll have you naked across the bed, I think, and take it from there."

She fumbled out of her clothes, turning and prostrating herself across the bed, her legs spread well apart and her breasts hanging heavily down.

His hands caressed her bottom and reached beneath her to briefly fondle her breasts, lingering around her nipples as they hardened readily under his touch."

Then his hands left her body and she braced herself as she heard him undressing and moving into position behind her. The belt whistled through the air and Julia rose up on her toes to meet it, feeling the heat of lust surging through her as it smacked hard into her taut flesh.

Thwack!

Thwack!

Thwack!

Without pause and with an almost unbelievable ferocity the blows whipped into her upthrust backside. She gasped aloud at the exquisite pain, pushing her twitching buttocks higher to meet each stinging stroke until Charles dropped the belt and bent close to her. His fingers traced along the broad, rapidly reddening welts and she squirmed and gasped out loud as he pressed harder, his touch further inflaming her hot stinging flesh.

Her sex was open and inviting, her nipples hot hard buds of desire.

She wanted his hands on her breasts, his throbbing cock thrusting deep inside her while she writhed beneath him. Between her thighs she could feel herself warm and wet, the lips of her sex quivering and twitching as he fondled her. He bent closer, his face almost alongside hers. His hard, throbbing cock slipped easily between her parted thighs and probed against those yearning lips.

She gasped aloud as he pushed slowly into her and he leaned closer, his face alongside hers.

"Did you say something, Julia?"

She squirmed and wriggled as his hands closed around her breasts, squeezing and fondling her tender flesh. His belly was pressed hard up against her stinging backside as he penetrated her fully, and she twisted her head around to face him, an expression of pure bliss on her face.

"Ahhhhh, yes, that's perfect, just perfect, MASTER."

Now we give you a short preview of one of our forthcoming titles: JANE AND HER MASTER by Stephen Rawlings

A decade ago that master of the classic S/M novel, P.N.Dedeaux, gave us *AN ENGLISH EDUCATION*, a version of Charlotte Bronte's JANE EYRE, in which he peeled away the prudish coverings required by the reading public of the day, to reveal what scholars had always recognised, the seething mass of cruelty and masochism that heaved beneath. In his preface Dedeaux points out key passages that reveal the thinly concealed sadism of Jane's treatment.

Jane refers to Rochester from first to last as 'my Master', and in this powerful and harrowing sequel to *An English Education* 'Stephen Rawlings' develops this theme further in a way that could not have been done in Victorian times and is daring even today.

I cannot say that my arrival at Thornfield Hall was an occasion of unmixed pleasure. True the house itself was pleasing enough, and I was looking forward with some considerable excitement to meeting my new employer and my charge, but I looked back too, to the manner of my departure from Lowood School, where I had been eight years a pupil, two of them as pupil-teacher, since my haughty Aunt, Mrs Reed, had banished me from her home at the tender age of ten.

For all those years I had served and suffered under an iron discipline and a rigid rule, enforced with severity by all the staff of that establishment but, above all, by the Rev. Mr. Brocklehurst, its Patron and ultimate source of all authority. Such formative, and reformatory, exercises, performed upon our bare buttocks with cruel rods, had extended right up until the moment of my departure to take up the Governess position I had been offered as a result of the advertisement I had placed in the County paper. At eighteen years, though slight of frame, I was woman grown and ready to set off into the wide world outside Lowood.

That morning Mr Brocklehurst had sent for me and delivered me a lecture on how to comport myself in the great world outside

the school and, to reinforce his point, and serve as a remembrance, for days physically, years mentally, as severe a whipping as any I received at his hands, and he had often whipped me to both blood and tears; a full two dozen, taken over the board, my feet parted so widely that I had to go up on my toes, the rod slicing in from beneath, the last four delivered 'short', so that the cruel tip whipped in and bit into my most tender and intimate woman's parts, where they pouted back between my spread thighs. As it was, I climbed into the coach, my buttocks throbbing and bleeding, my vulva aching, to sit on them for hours as we crossed the county to the distant house that I would henceforth call home. You may imagine that I was very glad to descend, my legs stiff, my gait uncertain, hoping that the blood that had oozed from my welts had not stained my gown right through.

It was dark when we came to the hall, but I could still make out a long lowish building of three stories, a light showing in one curtained bow window.

Trying to walk with something like a proper poise for a young woman of refinement, and succeeding in producing something nearer to what one might expect from a lame cow, for he had hurt me deeply and my wounds had stiffened from the long journey, I crossed the paving in front of the house and knocked at the great oak door of the hall, to be answered by a pert maid.

As Leah, as I soon found was her name, preceded me, I observed her firm, large haunches moving under the thin black stuff of her gown. I never saw a girl built more fairly for rod or strap, which was just as well, considering the forwardness of her demeanour which, I was sure, would oblige any proper employer to award her frequent and severe chastisement. These jouncey hinds led me to a modest sized, but comfortable room, where a lady of past middle age, but still sprightly, sat knitting before the fire.

"Good evening," *I said, dropping as polite a curtsy as my sore thighs and bottom would permit,* "you must be Mrs Fairfax. I am very happy to make your acquaintance."

"And I pleased to see you. Come to the fire, you must be cold after your tedious journey. Leah, fetch Miss Eyre some hot cordial, and some small thing to eat, then you may fetch something to warm yourself. I have not forgotten your need, my girl."

Forty minutes later and the world had become a more cheerful place. I was rested now, and warmed and fortified by the hot stimulant and the cold meats that Leah had produced. I had already entered into the beginnings of a cordial relationship with Mrs Fairfax, but as yet I had not met my pupil by reason of the lateness of the hour. Leah cleared away my tray, and returned bearing a thick strap of black leather.

"You will excuse me, I'm sure," Mrs Fairfax said, "but the hour grows late, and this impudent chit has earned herself a smarting behind by her insolence, and I do not like such matters to be held over to another day. A girl should take her welts to her bed, and seek to learn from them to do better the next day."

It is of course, a commonplace for mistresses to whip their servants for the betterment of their behaviour, and I made as if to leave.

"No," said the lady, "wait until she has had her dose, and she may show you to your room."

Accordingly I took my place again, and watched to see how matters would befall. Mrs Fairfax read the girl a stern lesson on the ease with which she might slip into familiarity beyond that proper in a servant, and the danger that, if not checked now, she might commit the same folly when gentry were visiting. She was then ordered to remove her gown, leaving her clad only in her stays over a short chemise. Leah was a comely country girl, very well built, round rosy cheeks above, and the same below, well set out before us as she was made to bend over a table, stretching across to grasp the far side. Her buttocks, though plump, were parted by her wide legged stance, and deeply cleft, so that her plump purse, framed in a glossy nest of dark curls, was clearly visible between the tops of her thighs, for she wore no drawers, as was common amongst the servant class at that time.

Mrs Fairfax rose from her chair before the fire and, taking the strap went to stand behind the bending girl. Now that she stood I could see that, despite the fact that she was no longer young, yet she retained a wiry leanness that suggested that this might be no gentle swishing, but something the girl might have reason to fear, as indeed she did, for the fatty halves of the buttocks twitched and flinched as the mistress approached.

Clearly this scene had been acted out before, probably many

times, for the girl was of that irrepressible kind that will always exceed her station if not checked, and then only mend her manners for as long as the bruise in her bottom are sore enough to remind her of her failings. Mrs Fairfax lifted her rigorous right arm and brought the strap down with a whistling sound, to wrap itself round the full curve of the generous hinds, printing a scarlet band across them like an exaggerated and burning version of the equator on the schoolroom globe.

Leah squealed and wriggled, until silenced and stilled by the mistress's sharp command, then jerked again as the strap descended to paint its fiery band across the Southern hemisphere of the gluteal globe. At regular intervals, six more snapping cracks, six more squeaks and yelps followed, until all Australasia was coloured with the red of Empire.

"Mercy," the girl howled, "have mercy Mistress."

"Hush you silly girl," Mrs Fairfax replied, "you know you have a dozen due you, and there are four more to come. Brace back your thighs, for I intend that they shall receive the benefit of your remaining stripes."

If she had squealed before, now she shrieked, as the merciless length of heavy leather lashed the backs of her solid white thighs, leaving the top four or five inches on either side quite as red as any part of the South Seas above. When it was done the girl lay on the table, wracked by sobs.

"Let that be a lesson to you," her Mistress declared, "now stop snivelling and put on your gown. Miss Eyre is fatigued from her long journey and needs her bed."

Still snuffling the girl did as she was bid, and presently showed me into a small but comfortable room, where I bid her good night, and advised her to think twice before she next let her impudence show.

"Indeed, I will Miss," she replied, "for my poor bottom hurts so, I doubt I shall find much comfort in my bed."

I too, I thought, as the girl departed, still sniffling, and grasping her tormented bottom in her hands as she left, for I was very conscious of the soreness in my own haunches, and, especially between my thighs, where Mr Brocklehurst's whalebone 'soko' had wounded me deeply but, in the event, my fatigue was such that it soon overcame all my hurts...

Silver Moon   Silver Mink

Silver Moon
ISBN 1-897809-01-8 Barbary Slavemaster *Alan Aldiss*
ISBN 1-897809-03-4 Barbary Slavegirl *Allan Aldiss*
ISBN 1-897809-08-5 Barbary Pasha *Allan Aldiss*
ISBN 1-897809-14-X Barbary Enslavement *Allan Aldiss*
ISBN 1-897809-04-2 Bikers Girl *Lia Anderssen*
ISBN 1-897809-17-4 Bikers Girl on the Run *Lia Anderssen*
ISBN 1-897809-11-5 The Hunted Aristocrat *Lia Anderssen*
ISBN 1-897809-07-7 The Training of Samantha *Lia Anderssen*
ISBN 1-897809-05-1 Bound for Good *Gord/Saviour/Darrener*
ISBN 1-897809-10-7 Circus of Slaves *Janey Jones*
ISBN 1-897809-20-4 Caravan of Slaves *Janey Jones*
ISBN 1-897809-16-6 Rorigs Dawn *Ray Arneson*
ISBN 1-897809-23-9 Slave to the System *Rossetta Stone*
ISBN 1-897809-25-5 Barbary Revenge *Allan Aldiss*
ISBN 1-897809-27-1 White Slavers *Jack Norman*
ISBN 1-897809-29-8 The Drivers *Henry Morgan*

Silver Mink
ISBN 1-897809-09-3 When the Master Speaks *Josephine Scott*
ISBN 1-897809-13-1 Amelia *Josephine Oliver*
ISBN 1-897809-15-8 The Darker Side *Larry Stern*
ISBN 1-897809-19-0 Training of Annie Corran *Terry Smith*
ISBN 1-897809-21-2 Sonia *RD Hall*
ISBN 1-897809-22-0 The Captive *Amber Jameson*
ISBN 1-897809-24-7 Dear Master *Terry Smith*
ISBN 1-897809-26-3 Sisters in Servitude *Nicole Dere*
ISBN 1-897809-28-X Cradle of Pain *Krys Antarakis*
ISBN 1-897809-30-1 Owning Sarah *Nicole Dere*

All our titles can be ordered from any bookshop in the UK and an increasing number in the USA and Australia by quoting the title and ISBN Or they are available from us direct for £5.60 each (UK) or $9.95 (USA) Credit Cards accepted as EBS (Electronic Book Services) £.s are converted to $.s.

We also offer a free 20-page booklet of extracts and maintain a confidential mailing list in both Countries.